A.N. PAYTON

Meads and Deeds

First published by A.N. Payton Publishing 2025

Copyright © 2025 by A.N. Payton

This novel is entirely a work of fiction. The names, characters and incidents portrayed in it are the work of the author's imagination. Any resemblance to actual persons, living or dead, events or localities is entirely coincidental.

Edited by The Assist, LLC.

Cover by GetCovers

Trigger Warning: This book may contain sensitive topics such as murder, loss, violence, or other triggers. Please be aware of your limit as a reader.

First edition

This book was professionally typeset on Reedsy.
Find out more at reedsy.com

Contents

Hallow's Promise

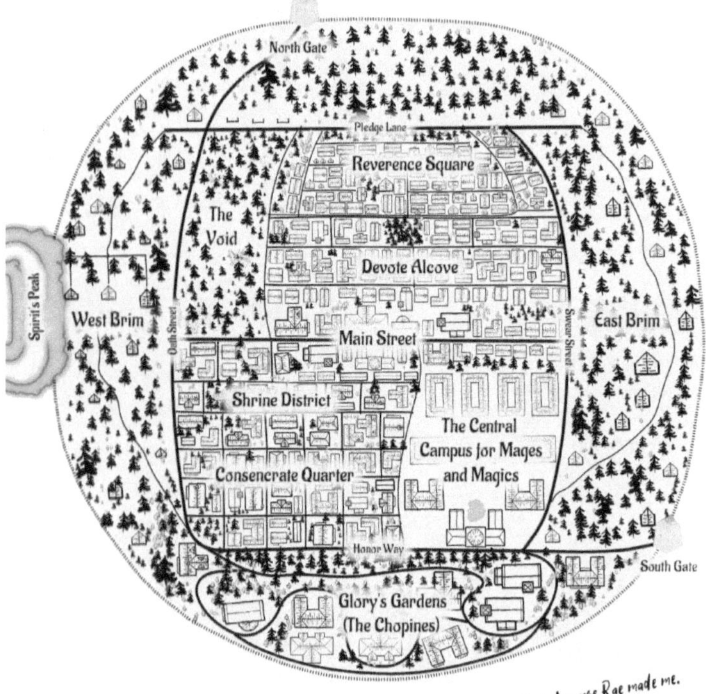

Chapter 1

"Alright, Sunshine." Valen's hand lingered at the small of my back. His touch sent tingles down my spine. "Just focus on the dead bug."

The bug in question was a shriveled, old beetle the mercenary had dug out of the herb garden at the back of my cottage. Metallic green and blue hues blended along its hardened back, fading into the abdomen and exposing a handful of little legs sticking straight up into the air.

I sucked in a deep breath. My magic—the specific flavor of power that craved life and death—uncoiled from my gut. It felt slow, lazy, like drudging up from leagues beneath the sea. I ground my teeth and poured more effort into awakening it.

"Keep breathing," Valen said softly.

That was easy for him to say. He wasn't the one attempting to persuade an anchor to rise from the bottom of a magical sea floor.

Sweat broke along my forehead. I wrestled with the magic, urging it to surface, aiming at the dead thing before me.

"Almost there."

I hated the beetle. My chest burned while I gasped for air. My arms trembled from their perch on the tabletop beside the couch in my living room. It certainly wasn't the bug's fault that my magic refused to surface since I'd brought Valen back from the dead two weeks ago. But my mind didn't care—I hated the beetle more than anything else at that moment.

A coil of ice crept along my arms. I didn't break my concentration from the desecrated target, but if I turned to Valen, I knew his eyes would be dark and focused as he wielded his power effortlessly.

The power he'd gotten from me, years ago.

The moisture on my brow cooled, and my next breath came easier. I continued tugging the power upward, a heavy weight against a strong current, but felt refreshed from Valen's magical touch.

Finally, a piece of my magic broke through the surface. I clung to the edges as it tried to sink back down and drew it into the daylight. It flickered through my cottage, licking the tonic and herbs gathered at the windowsill. Sparks flew from the fireplace as they danced along the flames.

"The beetle, Sunshine."

Oh, right.

I bit my lip and stared at the bug. Power wrapped along the ceramic plate serving as a mourning dais, touching the edge of the dead creature.

It withdrew.

I growled as I pushed the magic forward. It didn't get to decide what lived or died—I did. And today, fate had given me a very dead, dried beetle to resurrect.

Magic neared the bug. It grew heavier with each command, as though tiring from the struggle. Even Valen's cold power refused to ease the effort of controlling it.

It slipped. The magic slipped from my mental fingers moments before touching the bug. It happily sank into the depths of my soul, where it immediately relaxed and faded.

"Damn it!" I smacked my hand on the table. The plate holding the dead bug clattered loudly, flipping the beetle onto the floor.

Bubbles jumped from his spot on the couch and blinked grumpily at me for disturbing his nap. Actually, the warplog looked a little like the beetle I'd just lost beneath the table. A cross between a rabbit and a large frog, the creature had smooth green skin, powerful hind legs, and liked to sleep on his back with all his legs in the air. Normally, I'd feel bad for disturbing him. Today, I only felt frustrated.

I dropped my head into my hands. A heartbeat later, Valen gripped my upper arms and pulled me against his chest. He ran his hands through my hair and whispered nothing at all into my ear.

He felt *so good*. He smelled like forest and springtime and felt as good as the summer sunshine on my skin. His body was still recovering from being kidnapped and tortured, but every day was better than the last.

Valen hadn't left my house since I'd brought him here after his . . . rescue. He'd woken up on my couch after I'd raised him from the dead, and he went to bed there every night. I'd invited him to join me in the loft, but apparently, he'd wanted to talk about things first—things he'd proceeded not to mention since that conversation.

Sometimes I woke up in the middle of the night and my mind refused to believe I'd kept Valen alive. I'd creep down the stairs and watch him in the soft firelight, just to make sure his chest kept rising and falling. If the mercenary knew about those midnight observations, he hadn't said a word.

His touch lightened, and I drew back enough to study his face.

"That was a good try," he said.

I snorted. "Don't lie to me just because I saved your life."

"There really isn't a better reason to lie to someone." His half-smile melted my heart. "But it's the truth. You can't expect perfection right away."

"I literally brought you back from the dead a couple of weeks ago. I sort of expected to be able to do that again."

Valen lifted his hand to my face. His fingertips ran along my jaw, and a whirlwind of ice slipped over my skin.

"I'd like to think you were more motivated to reanimate me than the dead beetle."

"You'd like to think that, wouldn't you?" This was so effortless—bantering with Valen, pretending everything in our lives hadn't changed.

But it had.

"You hadn't used your magic in years. When I died—" I flinched even though he said the word casually, "your emotions and adrenaline were running very high. It was easy to overcome the rusty shackles you forced on your power. But it's going to take practice to wield that whenever you please."

I hated the words he said, but I loved watching his lips move. They were full and perfect and looked positively delicious.

A little crease caught between Valen's brows. "Are you even listening to me, or are you just staring at my lips?"

My cheeks burned.

"Don't get me wrong," he kept going. "They're very nice lips. And you have every reason to keep staring at them."

Part of me wanted to smack the smirk off the mercenary's face, but another part very much agreed with what he said.

When I didn't answer, Valen's gaze shifted. He traced his fingertips along my jaw and trailed them into my hair. I let my arms wind around his neck and pulled his chest against mine. We fit just right.

Valen ducked his forehead to mine. He'd stopped there so many times, and I was sick of it. I wanted him—all of him.

"Rae," he sighed.

"No." My tone was stern, and maybe some of that anger slipped through because Valen's eyes darkened and the temperature dropped. "You only use my name when you're being serious, and I don't want to be serious right now. I want more, Valen."

"There's so much we haven't discussed yet."

"You keep saying that, then you don't bring up anything to talk about."

Dark lashes lined his crystal blue eyes. His nose fit straight and smooth above those lips, all cradled by a sharp jawline that tightened as he clenched his teeth. "I'm trying to give you time to process everything. You rescued me from a situation that would leave a normal person with trauma—and you're not normal, Rae. You watched me die and brought me back from the dead, which has exposed your location to the king of Erline—who is going to want you back. And you've welcomed the rebellion to your doorstep, along with supporting a sheriff that has declared Hallow's Promise to be a sovereign kingdom. In case you had any doubts, that is a lot to process."

I guess when he listed everything, it did sound like a lot. But he'd left out all the important parts—like the fact that I really wanted to kiss him.

"Valen." I grabbed his hair in both of my hands and held his head against mine. He pressed against my hold, but didn't break it. I was stronger now, thanks to all the sword fighting, but he could easily escape if he wanted to. "I don't care about any of that. If you don't kiss me now, you need to find somewhere else to sleep because you're driving me crazy."

He blinked, and when he looked back to my face, shards of ice cut through his eyes. Tendrils of smoke oozed around our feet, running along my legs, and wrapping with my own magic that burned hot.

Valen shifted his hold. The hand around my waist became binding, pressing me closer to him. He grabbed my hair in his fist and tilted my head back. A sound escaped my mouth, half groan, half plea.

His lips pressed against my neck. I closed my eyes. Cold smoke and burning flames lingered where our skin touched. Valen's lips parted, and his tongue edged along my skin. A coil of need and desire unraveled in my gut, so opposite of the unyielding necromancy I'd been trying to command. This was effortless.

He worked his way up my neck. The smoke grew thicker. My body turned softer in his arms, consumed by fires winding through my nerves.

Valen held my head still. His gaze swept over my face, finally lingering on my lips. His lips parted, and he lowered his head.

A little chime sounded in my head—a warning from my wards that someone had entered my property.

I gasped. "No."

Immediately, the mercenary paused. The smoke and chill faded. He held me, but his grip loosened.

"No, don't stop." I pulled his hand tighter around me.

The mental sound came again—more of a horn and less of a chime.

Valen's brow pinched. "You're sending mixed signals, Sunshine."

"It's nothing, don't stop." I tried to pull him closer, but the man remained unmoved.

"Are you sure?"

"Yes, yes, I'm sure. Please, hurry up."

"Hm." He ducked his head back down, a bit of a laugh coloring his words. "That's what every man wants to hear."

I closed my eyes again. I wanted to savor the moment. Our first kiss, the first time he'd held me like this, the way his body felt in my arms. His strength pushed against me, a threat and protection at the same time. I wanted both—I wanted him all.

Someone pounded on my door.

Valen froze. I refused to open my eyes.

The knocking came again.

"I think someone's at your door," Valen said, his breath brushing my ear. More shivers cascaded down my spine.

"Ignore them. They'll go away."

A new voice shouted, "I bring news from the Marshal!"

"Sounds important."

"It's just my boss. He can wait." I would watch the world burn before I left this moment.

Valen pulled me in. He slipped his fingers beneath the hem of my tunic and groaned at the contact between our skin.

"Listen to me, Sunshine. I've waited a long time for this moment, and I refuse to be interrupted. When I finally get to have you, it will not be with a messenger at the door and your mind on any distractions. It will be slow, consuming, and will end with you screaming my name."

Oh. *Oh my.*

"Now, go see what the marshal wants because the sooner you find out, the sooner we can get back to this."

I tried to find my tongue, but I had swallowed it at some

point. All I managed was a half grunt as Valen detangled me from his body and directed me toward the intruder.

I stumbled to my own front door. From the rear of the house, the washroom door opened and slammed closed with a sharp snap. Valen must have been more frustrated than he'd appeared.

The constable at the door staggered when I pulled it open. His eyes widened as he glanced at me, then looked quickly down at his feet. I put my hand in my hair. Big tangles caught my fingers, and a blush heated my face. The constable probably guessed what activity I'd just been doing.

"How can I help you?" I asked, aiming for nonchalant and probably falling short.

"Um . . . the marshal has requested your presence at a death scene. He requires assistance as soon as possible."

My first kiss with Valen was interrupted because someone had to get murdered.

Maybe the moment didn't have to end yet. If I had enough time, we could finish what we'd started before this constable rudely interrupted.

"Give me the location and tell Leof I'll be there in an hour or so." Valen had promised to take his time. Was an hour long enough? I had no thoughts beyond the butterflies fluttering in my stomach.

"It's not Sheriff Leof, ma'am. And the marshal is requesting an immediate response."

I froze. Right, Leof was the sheriff now. He wasn't investigating simple murders—he was navigating the political nightmare of running a sovereign country, harboring a coveted fugitive, and rallying a rebellion.

"Who's the new marshal?" I asked, afraid to hear the answer.

"Marshal Castor, ma'am. I have the location right here." The constable handed me a piece of parchment, but I didn't reach for it. My mind couldn't comprehend what I'd just heard. Castor hated me. Why would he call me in for an investigation?

Valen moved beside me and accepted the card. I glimpsed a few words of the scene location before he pulled it inside.

"Tell Castor we'll be right there."

Chapter 2

Castor was a tall, broad-shouldered man with a soft face and even softer brown eyes. I could say he was handsome—if he weren't such an asshole. The marshal badge—which Leof refused to wear when he held the position—shone brightly on his chest in the springtime air.

We approached the marshal and his cluster of constables. Valen walked close enough that our arms brushed, and every contact sent a new flutter in my stomach. I very much wish we hadn't been interrupted.

Castor glanced at us, but didn't stop his conversation with the constables. That was fine with me. I got paid whether he talked to me or not.

Valen wasn't looking at Castor. His heavy gaze looked ahead, where the city wall rose from the depths of trees. This area of forest sat between the North Gate and Pledge Lane, and was mostly unoccupied except for a few more nomadic individuals.

"What are you looking at?"

Valen turned back to me. "Nothing." A half smile settled on his face, but tension pulled the corner of his eyes. He was hiding something.

I narrowed my eyes at him. Once we finished with whatever

Castor needed, I'd make the mercenary tell me what he'd seen. I refused to have secrets between us ever again.

"About time you got here." Castor stepped between Valen and me. He smelled like mint and lye—an odd blend of sharp and sweet. He studied the mercenary. "I don't remember inviting you."

"Consider my presence a gift." Valen winked. "You're welcome."

While I smothered a chuckle, Castor appeared less than happy. His lips twisted, and I worried that his next sentence may result in swords being drawn, but he leaned back. He didn't bother entertaining Valen anymore, instead turning toward me.

"You're probably wondering why I called you," he said.

I shrugged. "I figured it had something to do with a crime."

He lifted his lip. "Trust me, if there was anyone else, I would have called them. But apparently, you're the only freak that likes to play with dead things in this town."

"Oh, wow, and I wonder why you don't have a partner."

Castor turned red, and I feared his eyes might pop out of his head. "Just go in there and look at it. The sooner you leave my scene, the better."

It? "You mean the body?"

He waved his hand. "I'm not even sure it is a body. Go between those trees. Not even *you* can miss it."

Valen and I shared a glance, and I shrugged. If Castor didn't want to return to the scene, it was probably pretty bad. Luckily for him, pretty bad was normal for me.

It only took a few steps for the ashy smell to overwhelm the spring air. Even before we parted a perimeter of trees and tumbled into a mostly open field, I knew there had been a fire.

Flickers of gray specks rained from the decaying, burned bark that surrounded a circular area of trees and exposed a clearing. Smoldering stumps where proud trunks recently stood marked the lowly plots of demise.

I pulled my tunic over my nose and mouth, knotting it on the side. Valen did the same beside me. The cotton fabric didn't provide much protection from the ash and debris in the air, but it was better than nothing.

Between two crumbling piles sat the charred remains of what appeared to be a human body.

My stomach curled. The fabric dampened the smell, but burnt bodies were fragrant enough to evade most of the filter. They were a terrible combination of cooked pork and blackened sugar.

I crept closer to the victim. It wasn't surprising that Castor doubted the humanity of the shriveled form on the ground. They looked as bad as they smelled. I knelt beside the remains and studied them for a long time.

"What do you see?" Valen asked softly beside me.

I saw a lot of things irrelevant to my investigation. I saw they used to have short, blonde hair, which was still attempting to cling to a piece of the skull. Most of the clothing was gone, replaced with cracked and peeling skin. But these were not the things Valen or Castor needed to know. These were the details I would carry home with me and remember when the lights turned out and only the crackles of the fire kept me company.

"See how the limbs are curled up and in, toward the torso." I pointed to the corresponding areas as I talked. "That's a classic position in a fire-related scene. The muscles constrict in the heat and draw the limbs into a fetal position. That occurs whether the individual is alive or dead during the fire, so it doesn't tell us much. But the trees—that's a different story."

I stood, leaving the dead to their rest for now, and approached one of the burnt trees in the circle.

"There's some interesting burn patterns on the trunks." I hovered my finger over a darkened area that ate a good chunk into the bark. "This fire burned hot, but not long enough to go all the way through the trees on the perimeter." I guessed the distance to the stumps in the center of the burnt area. "But it didn't have any trouble consuming the ones in the middle."

"What does that mean?"

I tapped my finger on my chin. "It means that the center of this circle was hotter than the edges. I need to get a little farther out."

Valen trailed behind me. I walked out to the next tree, pulled off my face covering, and put my nose against the slightly less burned bark. It smelled of fire and ash. I went to the next tree and sucked in a big whiff. Hm, also normal post-fire smells.

The mercenary didn't speak while I bounced from tree to tree and smelled them all. He kept quiet when I lingered on one trunk a little longer, making sure that I accounted for all the scents before moving on.

I wished Leof was here. His werewolf nose deciphered scents far better than mine. But I hadn't confronted the new sheriff since I'd chosen another man over him—and thrust the responsibility of a sovereign kingdom onto his shoulders. Soon, I'd have to talk to the man. I just hoped he forgave me.

And I wasn't ready to face the consequences if he did not.

It didn't take a werewolf's nose to know that the fourth tree stank. A strong, bitter scent flooded my lungs as soon as I inhaled the air from the bark. I coughed and sputtered, making Valen chuckle, which diminished the glare I sent him as I hacked some more.

"When are you going to tell me why you're sniffing the trees?"

I wiped away the tears that were pooling in my eyes from the strong scent. "I'm not a scent mapping expert, but I think some kind of accelerant was used to start this fire. It burned so hot in the center because that's the most concentrated area of the accelerant, but it also burnt away whatever was used to start the fire. Less of the accelerant was applied out here, which is why these trees are still standing. And this tree stinks."

"You learned all of that by sniffing a few trees?"

My brows creased. "Well, no. There's a distinct burn pattern from the inside of the clearing toward this perimeter edge. And due to the heavier concentration of damage in the center, I'd expect that the fire started at or near the body. Since I'd narrowed down the point of origin and determined the absence of accidental fire-starting materials, that left very few options besides arson with an accelerant."

Valen stepped toward me. He cupped my face in his hands. "You, Sunshine, are truly remarkable." Warmth crawled up my chest and stole my breath.

"Thanks," I murmured. "I need to tell Castor what I've concluded, and he needs to get this body to Alivia." The mortician would probably be thrilled to get a shriveled up body to study. "And I need to collect a sample of the bark."

"Let me get the constable. You . . . collect your bark."

I smiled. I loved that Valen understood my work. "He's the marshal now, remember?"

Valen just snorted as he walked away.

I studied the burn line along the trees. The sample needed to contain remnants of the accelerant so I could run some tests, but areas with too much burning wouldn't give me any results. The damage crawled along the trunks and faded near the towering city wall. One tree had ash climbing halfway up its base before petering out below the branch canopy. It appeared to be in the correct range where some accelerant may still linger on the wood. I stepped closer, putting me beside the stone wall.

A shadow jumped over the top of the wall—easily clearing the twelve-foot structure. They landed on all fours and their hands pressed into the charred dirt.

I blinked. My mind didn't quite believe what I'd seen, even as all the nerves in my body vibrated with sudden alarm.

The shadow slowly stood, revealing a man in a very familiar black cloak with the hood pulled over his face.

Familiar—because I'd once worn the same one.

Dark eyes locked on me as he stretched to a ridiculous height—taller than Valen. A spark danced in his gaze, and he smiled.

"Drayven," he said. I flinched. I hadn't heard that name in years and had hoped to never hear it again. "I've come to take you home."

He lowered the hood and held out his arms as though inviting me to an embrace. One sleeve shifted up, revealing the dark outline of a dagger tattoo.

My heartbeat pounded in my throat. I drew my sword—which immediately started leaking smoke tendrils across the forest floor—but my hand shook. For weeks, I'd imagined all the possibilities and worst-case scenarios of what could have happened if I hadn't used my magic—if Valen had died. Looking at it in the face made me realize I hadn't really taken a moment to think about the whole truth of my decisions.

The king knew where I was, and he'd sent this Provider to

collect me.

Chapter 3

The man circled me. His gaze darkened as the smoke spilled from my sword. The misty tendrils waved in the air, only half obeying my mental commands. Similar to my necromancy, the smoke proved difficult to wield since I'd brought Valen back to life.

The Provider tapped one pale finger against his chin. "No one mentioned this in the briefing. You've learned some new tricks."

I spun the blade and sparkling sunlight reflected onto his face. "That's not all I've learned."

"So I see." His voice sounded flat, although those weary eyes didn't budge from my face.

Foreign magic thickened around me. The king of Erline collected powerful magic users and broke their will until they served only him. Whatever power this stranger possessed, it meant bad news for me.

I reached for my necromancy as his dark magic continued to strengthen. Nothing—that anchor dragging it into the bottom of my soul remained as heavy as before.

Fine. I would rely on my sword and sheer luck—like usual.

The ground shifted beneath me, and my knees trembled. I

didn't take my eyes off my opponent. Turns out it didn't matter, because suddenly the earth pulled beneath my feet, and I landed on my butt. Hard.

A deep noise came from the Provider as I quickly found my footing—a laugh, I realized, a terrible, broken laugh.

"You've had five years, Drayven, and you're as clumsy as a newborn fawn. I'd expected more of a challenge." He gathered his power again. Vibrations rattled through the ground and buzzed up my legs. He could win this fight just by knocking me over again and again.

I clenched my teeth and kept the sword in one hand at midguard, my spare hand stretched out to balance during his next strike.

"Funny," I said. "You know a lot about me, but I don't know anything about you. Seems your precious king didn't care enough to talk about you."

My taunting seemed to work as the Provider grunted and flung his power out, strong but sloppy with anger. The ground rocked again, taking all my focus to avoid stabbing myself with my sword. That would be embarrassing.

"The Highest will shower me in praise when I deliver his most precious item."

I snorted, sidestepping his next quake. "I forgot about all the *Highest* crap. Thanks for that terrible memory."

I actually heard his teeth grind together. Ouch, he was going to get a headache.

"You know nothing of what the word means." A weight sunk into the air around me, and a crackle groaned beneath the earth. Uh oh, I'd really pissed him off. "His Highest took you in as nothing more than trash from the streets and molded you into a great power. I will bury you, leaving enough oxygen to keep you alive, until you scream for mercy from the grave, and then you will apologize for your wrongdoings at the king's feet."

"Um . . . no thanks." I scrunched my lips involuntarily. Being buried alive as a form of torture sounded less than pleasant. "I actually have other plans for today."

The Provider's eyes widened, and his mouth sort of opened and closed. Aw, I'd already stolen the words from his lips. Now, I just needed to take his head off his neck.

I lunged forward, but I had to give the guy some credit—he was fast. I'd managed two steps before the ground tore open at my feet and I stumbled into a gaping hole.

Wet dirt slapped against my palms as I landed at the bottom of a ditch. The walls shook, trying to swallow me inside a dirt coffin. Not good. I scrambled for a perch, but my grip slipped off the muddy sides.

The Provider laughed again.

That did it. Nobody got to laugh at me anymore. At least, nobody except my closest friends.

I jabbed my smoking sword into the side of the wall, took two steps back, then sprinted forward. I lunged up the wall, digging my nails into the dirt, and bared my leg against the sword for more traction. The sharp edge cut at my leather trousers, but didn't pierce the fabric. The metal grew hot against my skin— the blade wasn't happy with its stepladder role.

The opening of the pit narrowed, and the Provider's tongue poked through his lips while he tried to urge the earth to close faster. It seemed once he started a task with his magic, he couldn't stop until he completed it. Good to know. I glanced back into the hole. Smoke now filled the space enough to cloud the bottom.

I scrunched my nose and squinted at one specific arm of

smoke. It coiled lazily at the end, flicking back and forth.

Come on, work for once.

The misty arm floated upward. Yes, yes . . . It caressed the side of the sword, seeming to savor the metal along its fleshless touch.

And the hole continued to close.

I pushed more magic into the smoke, but Smoke Wielding wasn't the same as necromancy. Applying too much magic turned the smoke too quickly and erased any semblance of control. It was more like fine-line painting and less like broad brushstrokes.

The smoke wrapped around the blade and tugged it effortlessly from the dirt wall. I was sweating while trying to maintain control. Slowly, the smoke tendril flicked my sword over the side of the trench wall.

I snatched the blade. My Smoke Wielding wasn't pretty, but it got the job done.

The Provider yelled as he poured more magic into the ground to prepare for his next attack. I couldn't let him trap me again—that had already been too close.

The sword jerked in my hand. I stumbled with its tug, bumping into a charred tree trunk.

Ah, of course. He could open the earth, but couldn't swallow me if I wasn't *on* it.

"Thank you," I told the sword as I stuffed it back into its sheath. It buzzed contently against my back.

I scrambled up the tree before the Provider aimed his next volley. The bark was cracked, but the thinner branches remained secure. My hands stained black as I climbed, and ash sprouted into my face. I hadn't replaced my face covering, and breathing in all these toxins probably wasn't great for my lungs.

Then again, breathing buried-alive-air probably wouldn't be good either.

The thin pine needles didn't offer many places to hide once I reached the upper limits of the branches. I would have very little besides a high-ground advantage to take down the Provider.

"Too afraid to fight me, little bird?" He mocked me, and the insult stung because it was so unnecessarily mean to birds. I, personally, once knew a giant bird that could have pecked this man's head off with barely a second thought—although Whiskers preferred the shape of a quaint hoglet these days.

I jumped along the branches. "Of course not," I bit out and studied my position. "I'm just looking for something first."

"And what, exactly, might that be?"

My next leap put me above the Provider's head, slightly in front of him. He craned his neck to keep me in sight, which meant he didn't see the smoke wrapping around his feet.

And this time, it wasn't mine.

Valen's smoke crawled more confidently than my hesitant strands. It flowed along the ground, consuming the space between Valen's hiding place and where the Provider smiled up at me.

One soft wisp circled the Provider's ankle. I ground my teeth. Valen was going to steal my kill.

"You can't hide anymore, Drayven. The king has demanded you return to him alive—he did not specify in what condition."

I eyed the next tree over. The distance required a bit of a jump, maybe a leap of faith more accurately. I bit the inside of my cheek. Valen's smoke swirled higher. I didn't have much time.

"Would you consider stepping a little to the left?" I called down without looking, wondering how many bones would break if I missed my target branch.

The Provider decided he'd had enough of my crap. His face turned purple, his lips twisted, and the ground beneath my tree shook with a sad groan. He planned to sink me into the earth, tree and all.

I sighed and crouched. Waiting any longer wouldn't just give Valen my kill, it would also give me a cozy, dirt-covered coffin.

The limb groaned beneath my feet as I pushed off. I launched forward, barely suppressing a scream. The Provider tracked my arc from one branch to the next, his face still turning colors as the earth cried below our feet.

I grabbed the branch. It wasn't as strong or thick as the previous one, which was exactly what I'd wanted. The wood bowed with my weight, giving me a slow descent—right toward the Provider's face.

I drew my sword as I fell. It vibrated sweet whispers into my hand. The weight shifted on its own, matching my aim as I eyed the Provider's chest.

His eyes widened, realizing my plan moments too late. He'd committed his magic to sink the tree I had abandoned, and reeling it back wasn't an option until the earth finished splitting apart. Too bad he'd be headless before then.

My feet hit the ground and my jaw snapped shut, but the impact didn't alter my strike. The swing was beautiful. The tip of my blade cut into the Provider's chest, and his body flinched with the force.

Then, his head fell off his neck.

I blinked. Blood oozed from the wound while his heart tried to reconcile the suddenly missing impulses from the spinal cord. The Provider's body went slack on the end of my sword and hung rather pathetically.

Valen appeared from behind the Provider, a smear of darkness in the sunshine meadow.

I pulled the blade from the body and pointed the bloody tip at the mercenary. "You stole my kill."

Chapter 4

"That's a weird way to say thank you." Rivets of red streaked down his own sword. Our blades matched, sister swords. Mine had been a gift after solving our first murder together, when I thought fate was all that connected us. I recently learned that he'd known about my past since our first encounter, when he'd broken into my house in the middle of the night.

"How did you even know he was here?" I narrowed my eyes and studied the city wall, where Valen had been staring when we arrived. "You saw him earlier, didn't you? Then you used me as bait?"

He strode toward me, all the arrogance in the world caught in his half smile. I poked the sword tip into his chest, which paused his progress.

"Sunshine, you're never the bait." A shimmer went through his eyes and straight into my stomach. "You're the most dangerous trap I could ever have set."

"Flattery will get you nowhere." I hoped he believed that, because flattery very much could get him anywhere he wanted with me. "Tell me."

He shrugged. "I felt a hint of magic when we arrived. I figured it would hurry things along if I appeared to leave you alone for a bit."

"Why didn't you show up when he first arrived and tried to make me a mud bed?"

Valen smiled. "I was watching the show."

I lowered the sword—I wouldn't use it anyway, and we both knew that. I studied the additional dead body we'd added to the crime scene and wiped my forehead with the back of my hand.

"We need to get rid of this guy, preferably before Castor shows up. I can go get Bubbles. I'm sure he'd enjoy a snack."

The smugness slipped from Valen's face. "Bubbles is probably full."

I snickered. "That warplog is never full."

"Well . . . You can try, but he's eaten three people in the same number of days. He's probably not going to want a fourth."

"I . . . I'm . . . What?"

He turned from me and wiped his sword across the Provider's cloak. I should have done the same, but my mind twisted around his words.

"Valen."

He paused and at least had the decency to grimace. "I've already killed three Providers from the capital and fed them to Bubbles. You can offer him another one, but I suspect it wouldn't go over well. He might throw up."

"You think I'm asking about the *warplog* right now?"

"Any good warplog owner would be. You wouldn't want him to have an upset stomach."

The fact that Bubbles' stomach had never been upset in his life was irrelevant. "Tell me about the Providers, Valen."

"I'd rather talk about you. Drayven, huh?"

I ground my teeth. My power fed on my anger, heat and

flames consuming my chest. "Tell. Me."

"Poor choice in names, if you ask me. It's like someone who'd never seen a child picked it out."

My given name scratched against my ears. I'd long ago left Drayven in the past, and its reappearance made me itch. Valen must have known that and decided to risk his own life by jesting about it.

My magic twisted and pulsed. I remembered how good it felt to have someone's life energy in my hands, to hold all that delicious power and consider every possibility it offered. I let those memories ooze into the magic, staining it with life and death and everything in between.

He kept going, as though he didn't feel his very existence hanging in the balance. "I mean, I see why you went with Rae now. It's short, punchy, and matches that sunshine personality." He winked.

The power pulsed. It had been unused for so long that the building tension made my head swim. It demanded release, and my unpracticed control couldn't gather the building strands. Valen was the source of my anger, so my magic appraised him as its target.

I didn't want to kill Valen, even if it might feel good for a moment. But all that heated power had to go *somewhere*. It layered across the ground, feeling for death, longing to ease the tension.

There, it whispered, *home*.

I gasped as my power flew out of me. As quickly as it came, the anger faded, my power humming in contentment. But where the magic left, a new, strong tether formed. It tugged at me, as strong as a physical touch. I looked down at my hands. Still holding the sword in one. The other looked normal. Despite the unfamiliar weight across my palms, I wasn't holding anything else.

"Good job, Sunshine," Valen whispered.

I turned to him. He smiled at me with the glow of a thousand stars. He looked at me as if I were the center of his world.

"What did I do?" I felt the magical leash, taunt and unfamiliar, but I didn't know what it connected me to, or what to do with it.

Valen grabbed my shoulders. His icy touch eased the panic, letting my head clear. He gently turned me to where the Provider's headless body now stood upright.

That leash pulled tight.

Part of me wanted to scream. After all, I'd watched Valen decapitate this man, and I might have stabbed his heart a little bit. But my power had always been life and death and left little room for fear.

"I did this." My voice held more awe than terror.

"I knew you could." Valen's breath danced down my neck and warmed most of my body. "I thought providing some deeper emotion might let your magic out to play." He'd taunted me into anger, into unleashing my magic subconsciously. He slid his hands down my arms, tingles and chills following every touch. "He's yours now, Sunshine."

Blood clung to the Provider's stumpy neck, and debris coated his sticky clothes. He didn't move at all—no sign of a heartbeat or a breath drawn. I hadn't raised him the same way I'd brought Valen back from the dead. No, I'd simply reanimated his body, while keeping his soul in whatever eternal damnation awaited those that served the king.

"I don't know how I did this."

"I don't either. Unfortunately, the power you gave me all

those years ago stopped short of reanimation. But I'm right here, and we'll figure this out together. Tell me what you feel."

We'll figure this out together.

When I escaped the capital about six years ago, I'd taken the life energy of five men and stuffed them inside a prisoner. I commanded the man—at that point, my puppet—to cut down anyone standing between me and the city gates. Normal people cannot survive the power of five lives, and when I finally fled Erline, I abandoned that prisoner to their death. I used him, knowing he would die.

Or so I thought.

I'd recently learned that Valen had been the man that freed me from Erline. He'd inherited some of my magic during the exchange, such as Smoke Wielding. Apparently, my magic liked to leak and turn anything I touched into something *more.* That's how I ended up with a magic potion wagon, a magic sword, and apparently a magic . . . significant other.

Valen should hate me for what I did to him. Instead, he wrapped his arms around me, faced down my terrible powers, and promised we'd get through this together.

My heart may explode.

"There's a leash," I said, avoiding all the other words. Those were for private, when Castor wasn't about to appear from the tree line at any moment. "It connects me and . . . it."

"What happens if you pull on the leash?"

I pressed my lips and mentally felt the edges of the tether. It seemed strong. I tugged slightly.

The body stepped forward.

I yelped, and my hold on the leash vanished. The man tumbled forward and whatever magic I'd lent him collapsed with my distraction.

"Damn it," I mumbled. I was never going to get this.

Valen's grip tightened. He caught my wrists and pulled them into my chest, trapping me against him. I tugged to test his strength against mine, and he held me effortlessly.

Gods, I loved it.

"You'll get it, Rae." He pressed a soft kiss behind my ear. "I promise."

Oh, gods. My legs were liquefying right here in the middle of an arson scene. I had fought for a place to be loved and accepted for exactly what I was. Hallow's Promise with Valen at my side, provided far, far more than I'd ever expected.

"Valen." His name was hope, desire on my lips. It tasted sweet and spicy and craved him—all of him.

He leaned down, eyes caught on my lips.

"That is disgusting." Castor's voice boomed through the forest. "Can't you two find a better place to lock lips? There's literally a dead body right here." He gestured toward the charred remains of the original victim. Valen shifted, exposing the Provider's body mere steps away.

Castor's eyes widened, then narrowed. "Great, there's another one. Do I even want to know what happened there?" He gestured vaguely toward us.

"No," Valen said, releasing me. I stepped a professional distance away, but even with my embarrassment at being caught, I mourned the loss of his arms.

Castor studied the dead Provider, the dagger tattoo marking his place among the king's ranks visible on his exposed wrist.

The marshal pointed at the dead guy. "I'm going to say *he* was killed during an act of upholding Hallow's Promise's sovereign separation from Erline. Is that a correct assumption?"

"Yes," Valen and I both declared in unison.

"Good." Castor nodded. "That's a lot less paperwork for me. Tell me about the burned body so we can get the hell out of these woods."

I recanted everything I'd learned about the scene—the arson, the accelerant, and the burn patterns.

"Did the fire kill him, or maybe the Provider did the deed?" Castor asked, a bit of hope obvious on his face.

I shook my head. "The Provider didn't have fire powers. More 'I'll bury you alive' type magic. I doubt they're connected. As far as the cause of death, you'll have to ask Alivia."

Castor visibly shook. "Fine. You can go. I'll let you know when Alivia decides to do the autopsy."

I hesitated.

"What?" he asked, not looking at me.

"Well . . . I'm honestly surprised you summoned me at all, much less that you'll want me at the autopsy."

Castor sighed. He looked around, grabbed my arm, and shuffled us into a more secluded area away from his constables. Valen moved to follow, but I shook my head. If Castor decided to be an ass, I was perfectly capable of defending myself. Besides, Valen owed me a kill.

Castor lowered his voice. "If you tell anyone I said this, I will deny it, and your job at the station will disappear." I did a little X over my heart with one finger, which only earned a more pissed-off expression. "You're good at this job. And I'm new. There's a lot riding on my first case, and I need it to go well. I need your help."

"Your will is my command, or something like that." I gave him a bow and followed up with a wink. His face was red by the time I spun around and blew him a kiss over my shoulder.

Valen caught my hand. His smoke wrapped around us.

"Wait!" I yelled before his magic made us disappear.

The shadows froze. "What?"

"I need my bark!"

I let his fingers slip from mine and ran to collect my sample with the sound of his laughter ringing in my ears.

Chapter 5

I still hadn't kissed Valen.

A little bubble of anger—which wasn't all that *little* anymore—grew inside my chest. Pretty soon it was going to burst through my mouth and release all kinds of nasty words I didn't really mean.

When we arrived at my house with my handful of bark intact, Krissa and Ilene lounged on my front porch. Once Valen established a residence at my house, and I refused to ask when he planned on leaving, I had to shift the wards to allow him to come and go as he pleased. Contrary to the tiny voice in my head, trapping someone inside my house would be wrong. Since I worked on the wards anyway, I also allowed Krissa and Ilene to enter alone without experiencing the Fire Crotch protection spell. Their presence on the porch was simply a result of the lovely weather.

But, rather disappointingly, I didn't want to kiss Valen in front of his sister, which meant I would continue to not kiss him.

Ilene was stunning, as usual. Her blonde hair twisted away from her face in delicate curls, sunlight adding a golden hue to the light shade. Blue eyes matched Valen's, framed by dark lashes and high cheekbones. She almost always wore a set of old armor, filled with dirt and reddish-brown stains I'd rather not look at too closely.

Ilene led the rebellion against the king of Erline. She had a variety of nicknames as their leader, most infamously the Phoenix Queen—although she thought up new ideas every day.

Krissa let her hand slip from Ilene's as we approached. She stood from the chair on my stoop—one I may, or may not, have put there specifically for her—and a little hoglet trailed on her heels. The creature looked at me with beady eyes when Krissa pulled me in for a hug. I didn't maintain eye contact. The hoglet—Whiskers—had the power to split reality apart and pull creatures from another dimension into our world. When he looked at me, I felt that unearthly power in his gaze.

While Krissa broke our embrace, Ilene didn't bother with pleasantries.

"We have been waiting a long time." Her armor rattled as she crossed her arms.

Valen smirked as he strode by his sister. The door to my cabin unlocked at his touch and released a flood of warm air, tinted by the rows of herbs drying in my windowsill.

"If I had it my way, you'd still be waiting," he said.

"What could be of more importance than the war?"

Valen sent me a glance over his sister's head. Heat billowed in the depths of his dark eyes, enough to make my cheeks burn. He looked away.

Krissa hadn't missed the interaction. She wrinkled her nose and mouthed, *Gross.*

"Someone died," Valen said. "Rae was summoned to the crime scene."

"Is it relevant to the war?" Ilene asked. She wasn't about to change the topic based on something as trivial as murder.

"No, but there was another Provider."

"Another?" Ilene tapped her chin with a slender finger. "They're becoming more brazen."

I rounded on Ilene. "You knew?"

She blinked blue eyes far too innocently. "Of course. I am well versed in the happenings of the capital. I also know they've been well disposed of." Ilene gestured toward the couch, where Bubbles lazily opened one eye. He didn't even manage to groan—now I knew it was because he was stuffed full of dead people.

Krissa eyed the warplog. He'd casually flung one undersized front leg across the pale length of a bone.

"Is . . . is that a piece of a human?" Her voice shook.

I blinked. Bubbles was happily curled up against a human humorous, which wasn't as funny as it sounded. Warplogs regurgitated the bones of their meals and chomped them into pieces to file down their continuously growing teeth. Apparently, Bubbles hadn't gotten to the chomping part yet.

"Of course not," I lied before stepping inside and pulling the bone away. The warplog remained unroused.

Krissa opened her mouth, but Ilene spoke first.

"Brother, I must speak to you in private." She grabbed Valen's arm and hauled him toward the rear of my cottage. The space was too small for any conversation to be private, but Krissa and I headed to the table near my front door to offer them the illusion.

A lot had happened in the few short weeks since we'd rescued Valen. Leof was the new sheriff, and I'd avoided him at all costs. I'd had the opportunity to choose between him and Valen, and, well . . . Valen was living with me now—whatever that meant.

But as the sheriff, Leof had declared Hallow's Promise as a sovereign kingdom, unruled by Erline's decree.

I had used my magic for the first time since fleeing the capital. The king had discovered my location and apparently sent his special pets out to capture me.

And those were just my issues. Krissa was dating the leader of the rebel army, who had moved her warfare headquarters into Krissa's apartment on the Central Campus of Mages and Magics. I'd been unfairly banned from selling tea on the school grounds, and if Dean Perthum discovered Krissa's after-hour activities, he'd probably ban her from campus, too.

"How's . . ." What do you even ask the girlfriend of a rebellion war leader? "The war?"

She smiled, her skin smoothing along her forehead. Krissa was, as usual, adorned in a plethora of colors. Besides the bright top and less than sensible floor-length skirt, she wrapped ribbons into her braids, and a vivid pink sash hugged her shoulders.

"The war is good, actually. Ilene has been busy managing the front line, but she's able to visit once a week or so. She has a witch that's good with transportation spells, so she's not wasting days traveling."

I nodded. The first time we'd met Ilene, she'd appeared in a beam of light. Hopefully she'd discovered more subtle ways to navigate.

Krissa continued to fill me in on the war-front—although I wasn't sure how much I wanted to know—and I put my bark on the table.

"Hold that thought," I told my best friend. I ventured into the kitchen, carefully creeping behind Ilene to avoid interrupting her whispered conversation with Valen, and uncovered a candle holder and a pair of metal tongs. "Okay, you can keep talking now."

But Krissa's interest in war updates had disappeared. She folded her hands together and tucked them beneath her chin. "Ooo, you're investigating a case?"

"Of course, I am. It's in the job title."

"Funny, Rebel Necromancer doesn't say anything to me. Neither does Disgraced Provider."

I sent her a look. "What about Ex-Best Friend?"

"You wound me." She put a hand over her heart but let out a laugh.

"I'm not sure how much help I'll be in this case. It's an arson scene, and there's limited analysis I can perform."

She eyed the supplies I was assembling. "It looks like you're going to try something."

I shrugged. "Some accelerants can burn different colors based on their composition."

"You're planning to burn the evidence you collected from the crime scene?"

"Yes. For science."

Krissa chuckled, but her sharp gaze watched my every move. "Tell me what you're expecting from the bark."

"I'm not expecting much more than this wood catching on fire. But theoretically, if the flames are green, that's indicative of sulfur in the accelerant. Pitch-based concoctions burn gold. Animal fat will be yellow."

"Yellow and gold sound awfully hard to tell apart."

"That's why *I'm* the Crime Investigation Expert." I winked.

She huffed and rolled her eyes. "More like Crime Investigation *Idiot*."

"Hey!"

I lit the candle with the flames dancing in the fireplace and set it into the metal holder. With the tongs, I carefully plucked the first piece of bark.

"This is a control piece. I pulled it from the same type of tree, but far away from the scene of the fire. It will show me what color untainted bark should burn."

The fire ate up the bark, emitting a soft light and amber colors.

I plucked up the test piece and carefully set it in the heated tongs. "This one should contain trace amounts of the accelerant." The wood looked the same as the last piece in the glow of the flames. Hopefully, enough of the substance remained for a meaningful test.

Krissa watched quietly—for once—as I hovered the wood over the candle. The flames licked along its victim, almost savoring it before igniting along the edges.

I should have been suspicious about her silence.

"Have you and Valen done it yet?"

My hands jerked suddenly, the flaming piece of wood bounced out of the metal tongs. I barely registered the soft green waves of flames before it sailed across my table like an emerald flag—announcing my embarrassment to the entire room.

The burning chunk landed on the floor near the door. The green tinge was even clearer now—revealing that sulfur had been the primary ingredient in the arson accelerant—but Krissa and I just stared at it. I was too stunned by her question and the fact that my face felt like it was on fire to smother the small flames. I didn't know Krissa's excuse.

"I'll take that as a no," she said.

I choked.

"You can't just ask that," I whispered harshly as logic finally returned to my brain. I grabbed a pitcher of water and circled the table, with Krissa close on my heels.

"Well, it's been a month. I was just wondering how things are going."

The liquid splashed across the ground. Probably overkill for the tiny piece of bark, but maybe it could douse the fire in my cheeks by proxy.

"Valen says he doesn't want to rush me after everything I've been through, and he wants me to have time to process. He's being a perfect gentleman about it all . . . and it's driving me crazy."

Krissa nodded. "You want him to ravish you."

The pitcher fell from my hands and crashed to the ground, spilling the rest of the liquid onto the floorboards. My lips sputtered, but nothing came out.

She raised her brows. "What? Every woman needs a good ravishing now and then. It's a requirement."

Oh gods, take me now.

I flicked my eyes toward the shadowed area of my kitchen. Valen and Ilene didn't glance our way despite the whole fiasco unfolding.

"Is that what you call it?" I grabbed the nearest towel and dropped to my knees, cleaning up the mess. "Tell me, how is your *ravishing* with Ilene going?"

Her cheeks turned pink this time, and she gave a very satisfying glance back toward the kitchen.

I didn't let her off the hook, though. "Is having the Phoenix Queen living in your house providing all the ravishing fantasies you've been lacking?"

"Scourge of Erline," Krissa said, flatly. She found another rag on the tabletop and plopped down beside me.

"What?"

"Ilene—she's going by the Scourge of Erline now."

I couldn't keep up with Ilene's self-appointed titles. "That's not my favorite."

"Mine either." Krissa shrugged. "But I'm not going to tell her that."

I also wouldn't tell her that. Ilene could pummel me to a pulp with her pinkie finger.

Krissa continued, "But it's been going really well. She's able to come home quite often from the front lines. Of course, she has lots to do when she is here, but . . . She's really good about prioritizing our time together."

A smile crawled across my face. *Home*, Krissa said. A place where the two of them felt safe together. My best friend deserved that, even if it came at the price of an armored warrior-goddess, and the word *ravish* becoming common vocabulary.

"I'm so glad, Krissa," I said. Oh no, my voice had that tight, high-pitched tone. And my eyes were burning from something far worse than embarrassment.

She glanced up at me. "Are you crying?"

"No! I just . . . it's still a little smoky down here. From the flames, you know." I sniffled, a totally normal response to cleaning up waterlogged bark ash from the floor. "But I am really happy for you and Ilene. I know things haven't been easy lately."

Krissa grabbed my hand. Her fingers squeezed around mine, and she smiled, sweet and innocent, wanting only good things for me.

"If he won't ravish you, maybe you need to ravish *him*."

Okay, scratch that. It wasn't innocence or well-wishes in her gaze. It was pure, unfiltered evil, and it needed to be purged.

I pulled my hand from hers and threw the sopping wet towel into Krissa's face.

She froze, mouth open, liquid streaming from the rainbow ribbons in her hair. With a loud squeal, she threw her own rag at me—missed—and followed it up with the towel she plucked off her head. The fabric smacked against my face, stealing my breath, and convincing an involuntary scream out of my lips.

The towel covered most of my vision, but I partially saw Krissa dragged out of the way, replaced by a vision of splendor in worn armor.

"Where is the threat?" Ilene wielded her sword low and dangerous, those beautiful blue eyes taking in every inch of my living room. "Tell me, love, and I will dispose of it immediately."

Krissa giggled behind her unnecessary hero. "It was just Rae. She threw a towel at my head."

Ilene straightened, but her blade didn't lower. "Do you wish for me to dispose of her due to that transgression?"

"Relax, sis." Valen pushed Ilene's sword down and the woman snapped upright, as though coming out of a trance. "They're just playing."

Her brow creased. "But they are not children."

"Could have fooled me." Valen stepped beside me. My mind immediately blurred, and my vision fuzzed at the edges. Really, there was nothing else worth looking at when the man stood so close and smelled so good. The rich evergreen and rain scent should have been illegal.

His power, raw and dark, crawled against my skin and set every part of me aflame. I vowed to never say the words out loud, but maybe Krissa was right. Maybe part of me craved a little ravishing.

Valen ducked his head to stare into my eyes. He ran the pad of his thumb beneath one eye, catching a little moisture clinging to the lashes.

"I have to go," he whispered.

Ah, ouch. My chest clamped so tightly that I had to resist the urge to rub over my heart.

"Ilene needs my help. I'll be back tomorrow. Will you be okay?"

I forced a smile, but it felt small and hollow. "Oh no, how will I ever fare without you? It's not as if I managed the rest of my life alone . . . Hm, wait a minute . . ."

His hands circled my biceps and all the sarcasm dropped from my voice. He pulled me closer, which I very much wanted him to do, and pressed a kiss against my forehead. It wasn't exactly the kiss that I wanted—one that would light up every nerve in my body—but it still felt good.

It felt safe.

He pulled back. "You'll wait for me?"

"Forever."

Valen smiled. Krissa and Ilene finished their own farewells. We walked them toward the door and stood side by side while they disappeared into darkness. A hint of Valen's smoke was the only sign they'd truly left at all.

"That's the part I don't like," Krissa said.

"We have a lead on the case now." That's right. Maybe talking about work could stop the ache in my ribs. "Tomorrow, you can help me question the sulfur suppliers in town."

"Yeah, that sounds good."

We both pretended not to see the other wiping their eyes as I closed the door and locked it.

Chapter 6

"There's two places that are licensed to sell sulfur in town." We reached the intersection of Pledge Lane and Oath Street, where it connected to the little dirt road that leads from my house in the West Brim. Leaves across the canopy swayed happily in the fresh spring air, which still felt cold inside my lungs.

Bubbles hopped beside me, and Whiskers strolled on Krissa's other side. They'd spent the night at my house, occupying Valen's usual place on the couch. It seemed like neither of us had a fondness for being alone anymore.

"Where's our first stop?"

"Dollups and Dashes."

Krissa's face brightened. "Oh, I love that place!"

Main Street cut across the center of Hallow's Promise. It held the largest buildings in town, except for the Central Campus for Mages and Magics. At this time of year, tourists populated Main Street in a thick swatch of chatter and excitement.

Except . . . today it was empty.

"Woah," Krissa said as we strolled along the cobblestone road. Shops displayed prominent lanterns illuminating open signs and the shopkeepers inside watched our path with wide, hopeful eyes. "It's completely abandoned."

A weight sunk in my chest. I had a good guess why the typical tourist season was suddenly depleted.

"We've become enemies of Erline," I said. "They've probably restricted travel to Hallow's Promise."

Down the way, Siren's Sorrow—an inn known for its pleasure in hosting unruly guests—appeared dark and quiet. I bit my lip.

"This is my fault."

If I hadn't become comfortable in Hallow's Promise all those years ago, none of this would have happened. These people's lives were impacted because I wanted a place to settle down and grow roots. Every time I decided to care about something, other people got hurt. This was no exception.

Krissa put her hand on my arm. "Did you establish an authoritative rule and sentence anyone with magic powerful enough to threaten your crown to an automatic death?"

"No, but—"

"Did you kidnap a child and force them to kill others to keep you alive?"

"No, but—"

"Do you force people to change their children's names to track the offspring of prior traitors to the crown?"

"Would you listen to me? Of course I didn't do that. But I brought the king's gaze here. He never would have punished Hallow's Promise if I had just kept running."

We arrived at Dollups and Dashes, but Krissa grabbed my arms before I pulled the door open.

Her chocolate eyes searched mine, and it felt like she looked directly into my soul.

"If you didn't come to Hallow's Promise, Gerrin's dark magic would have killed Leof last year. They would have hanged me for a crime I didn't commit. Kara would have been accused of murdering Adora when she never even knew her name. You are not a scourge to Hallow's Promise. You have helped all of us. Now, let us help you."

I shrugged from her grip. "I hear what you're saying, but it still feels wrong. It still feels like my burden."

"It can feel however you need it to, but don't let the lies consume you." She pointed to Bubbles. "That thing would certainly be dead without you."

He blinked at me and burped. Okay, she had a point there.

Dollups and Dashes welcomed us through a forest green door that opened into an outcrop of jars and glasses across several wooden shelves. The store was divided into sections—pigments and paints, healing supplies, spellcraft equipment, herbs and tonics, and a sort of haphazard other section where a tiny skull smiled down at me. I caught Bubbles eyeing the remains, but he turned away after deciding there was clearly no flesh left to eat.

A man I didn't recognize stood behind the register. He smiled when we walked inside, a sort of plastered expression that didn't meet his eyes.

"Good morning. How can I help you, ladies?"

"Hello, is Brynn out this morning?" The shop owner was a delightful young woman usually adorned in layers of gold jewelry.

"She's in River's Edge setting up the new shop. I'm Eleric, her cousin, and I'm just filling in while she sets up the new place."

I blinked. "Why is she opening a store in River's Edge?"

Eleric glanced out the windows over my shoulder. "You've probably noticed business isn't the same as last year. Brynn wants to keep the shop open in Hallow's Promise, but there's not exactly an income right now. She's hoping a second location can keep both stores open."

"Oh." It wasn't the brilliant response I wanted to have, but guilt and shame stopped any other words from forming in my mind. "Do you know when she'll be back?"

He shrugged. "I'm told to show up every morning until she tells me not to."

Krissa bumped my shoulder, apparently realizing that Eleric's revelations settled heavily on me. "Do you know anything about your sulfur supplies?"

The man grimaced. "I know we have some on the shelf. In the paints and pigments section, I think? Or wait, it might be in healing herbs. You can go look at the labels."

"Has anyone bought a large quantity of it recently?"

"Look, ladies, I'm trying to be here as little as possible. It's not exactly my dream job, you know? Brynn is family, so I'm happy to help her out, but I don't know anything about the stuff she sells. If you want to ask about moving a lot of stock, you should ask the night workers. They receive and ship the orders after the store closes, and they'd be the ones setting aside any special requests."

Ah, finally my brain woke up at this mention of a usable lead. "What are their names?"

Eleric scratched the back of his neck. "I don't know all of them. Sito and Veric show up when I leave for the night. There's at least one more I haven't met."

"Will they be here tonight?"

"We're closed tomorrow, but they'll restock the day after that. Assuming Brynn has enough money to order more stock, that is."

I smiled and tried to make my voice warm. "Thanks, Eleric,

that's helpful. If anyone shows up during your shift looking for a large quantity of sulfur, will you send a message to the sheriff's station for me? Ask for Rae."

"Did something happen? Are Sito and Veric in trouble?" He looked a little too excited about that.

"No one is in trouble." That I've figured out yet. "I just have some questions for them. But thanks for your help. Tell Brynn I said hi."

Krissa and I stepped away from the counter and meandered to the shelves.

"Which one do you think it was?" Krissa asked.

"What?"

"Sito or Veric? Which one do you think killed the guy?"

I glanced at Eleric, who was wiping down the counter with a sort of mindless expression that probably meant he was trying to hear every word we said.

"I can't possibly know whether either of them did it. We haven't even talked to them."

"My bet's on Veric. That's definitely a murderer's name."

Krissa continued dissecting the probability of the murderer's identity based solely on their names while I scanned the shelves. A bit of sulfur was stocked on the shelf with paints and pigments, but a much larger jar sat with the healing supplies. It was empty.

"I'm guessing they will be delivering more sulfur with the next restock because they're pretty much out on the shelves. We'll have to come back in two days and talk to the night staff."

"Ooo, I love a good interrogation."

"It's not really an interrogation because we don't have any reason to suspect them. They could be setting the order aside for another buyer."

"No, it's definitely Veric. I know he's our man."

"Thank you!" I called to Eleric as we left the shop. He responded with a short wave.

"Where to now?"

"The butcher's shop."

Krissa eyed Bubbles. "Good idea, he does look a little peckish."

The warplog looked anything except peckish. He was round—rounder than when I'd first found him—and was panting a little bit while hopping beside me. I wasn't about to tell Krissa he'd eaten three human bodies in the last week.

"He's fine," I said. "Sulfur is a common ingredient in food preservation. Matilda is the second licensed seller in town."

"Oh, that makes more sense, because Bubbles actually does not look hungry. He might even be a little fat."

"Krissa!"

"What?" She knelt closer to the warplog and stuck one finger into his round side. His gut pushed in, froze, then slowly expanded back out. He met my eyes with his beady gaze, and his tongue dashed out to lick over the surface of one eye. "I don't think that's rude. I'm just stating a fact."

I scooped him up. Oh my, has he always been that heavy?

"Don't listen to her. She doesn't know what she's talking about."

Bubbles had a double chin as he snuggled his head into the crook of my arm and settled in for a short nap. Fine, my warplog was a little fat, but it didn't matter. If anything, it made him even cuter.

Chapter 7

A bell jingled over the door of the butcher's shop, announcing our arrival. The store carried that metallic scent of blood I'd grown far too accustomed to. Stacks of meat were piled in a simple display at the front. Bubbles roused from his sleep, studied the rows of steaks, and started drooling. The creatures were insatiable.

The white sheet near the back of the room shuffled open, and a petite woman with dark hair emerged. Matilda's lips split into a grand smile when she saw us, but solely because she loved Bubbles.

"Oh, my sweet baby boy." Matilda put down a giant knife, pulled off her bloody apron, and headed toward Bubbles with her arms out. I relinquished hold of the warplog. The butcher shuffled him in her arms until his beady eyes stared at her with affection. "How have they been treating you? Here, I have something special I've been saving."

Matilda set Bubbles down, rounded the counter, and revealed a slab of meat wrapped in paper. She quickly unwound the ties with one hand. A foul scent filled the room.

"Oh ma guds," Krissa said, her nose plugged and eyes watering.

I didn't fare much better. The smell of decay was never pleasant, and my gut churned with displeasure.

Bubbles stared at the meat. He continued to drool, but his mouth remained tightly clamped.

Matilda frowned. She shook the paper and its unpleasant contents. "You don't want it, dear?"

Bubbles didn't shake his head, but he turned away and closed his eyes, which was the next best form of refusal.

Matilda scooped the warplog up and held him out in both arms to study his face. Bubbles opened his eyes a crack. He did not open his mouth.

"Is he feeling all right?" Matilda asked.

"I think he's fine." I certainly wasn't going to admit Valen had fed him three human bodies in the very recent past. Or that he was getting a little fat. "He's been eating a lot lately, maybe he's not hungry."

"Perhaps." She passed Bubbles back to me. He pressed his smooth skin against my arm and huffed in contentment. "Let me package this up and send it home for later."

Oh, goodness, she was wrapping up the vile meat slab in fresh paper.

"You don't have to do that, Matilda. I have some leftovers at home he'd be happy to eat."

But she waved my words away. "It's no trouble at all. Trouble would be keeping it in the shop. It spoiled days ago." Really? I couldn't tell . . . "If you're not here for Bubbles, dear, how can I help you today?"

"I'm actually visiting for a work-related reason."

Her capable hands paused as Matilda cocked a brow. "Work? Someone's been killed, then?"

"I can't share case details, but I was hoping to ask a couple of questions. You're listed as one of the commercial licenses for sulfur in the town, is that correct?"

"Oh, yes. We use it in the shop as part of the concoction to preserve the meat after it's cut. We also sell it to the farmers, who apply it to their crops and grasses. The insects don't like the smell, you see. More grasses mean more meat for us."

Krissa wrinkled her nose. "It sounds like there's a lot of people purchasing sulfur from you."

"Nobody's complaining when their meat isn't spoiling on the shelves," Matilda chuckled. "But I do keep a sales log, dear, if that would be helpful."

"Yes, Matilda, that would be wonderful if you'd let us look at the log."

"Of course, dear." She retied the bloody apron and disappeared behind the curtain again.

Krissa leaned her head toward mine. "I can't get the smell out of my nose. Are you really going to take that home with you?"

"No, I'm going to slip it into your bag and send it home with *you*."

"I've never had murderous inclinations before, but if I find that rotting meat in my bag, I may have to reconsider that stance."

Matilda returned with a leather book in her hands. She set it on the counter and flipped to the last page. "Here you are, all the sulfur sales this year."

My heart sank. There were dozens of business names scrawled across the parchment. It didn't matter that her handwriting was neat and legible. I'd never get through interrogating all those businesses alone.

"Would you like me to transcribe a copy? It'll take only a

moment."

"Matilda, you're an angel."

She laughed again. "There's a few people in my life that would beg to differ."

"You should take comfort in knowing they're all wrong."

A few minutes later, we aimed toward the door with my fresh list in hand. Bubbles was fast asleep, his little chest rising and falling against my arm. He didn't even stir when the bells over the door rang as Krissa pulled it open.

"Rae!" Matilda called back. "You almost forgot the meat!"

I froze. Krissa pretended to cough to hide an evil smile. But I spun back. I didn't have it in me to reject the beautiful gift Matilda had for Bubbles, even if it made my eyes water.

"Thank you so much," I said, accepting the package that uncomfortably squished against my hand.

"Have a good day, dear. Best of luck finding your killer."

I smiled and waved as the bells over the door settled behind us with a soft finality.

"There's over twenty names on that list," Krissa said as we rounded the corner away from the shop.

"You don't say."

"Oh, hush. I mean, we can't visit all those shops on our own. Unless you're planning to stop your extracurricular activities with the mercenary, then maybe we'd have time."

My face immediately lit up. "There are no . . . extracurricular activities."

"I know I should be happy about that because I've never cared much for Valen, but as your friend, I say this wholeheartedly: *bummer.*"

I scanned the list to avoid meeting Krissa's gaze while the blush still burned my face. Some of the places looked familiar, and there were a few I'd never heard of.

"I've been to North Gate Butcher before," I said.

"On the other side of town? Why?"

"It's where I learned about Whiskers and his true identity as the Nightingale. It's where Magnolia used to buy his food when he was a cat."

Krissa's gaze grew distant. "Maybe I should bring Whiskers nearby to visit, then. He takes Ilene's absence hard, too. Perhaps seeing a familiar face could cheer him up."

"You can always have Bubbles over for a play date, too."

Krissa laughed, and I joined in. Neither of our animal companions did anything except eat and nap.

But the laughter faded as reality set in. I wouldn't be able to talk to everyone required for my investigation. Not on my own, even with Krissa's help.

I sighed.

"You know what you have to do, huh?" Krissa asked, an understanding expression softening her eyes.

"Yes."

"There's only one person who has the resources to question that many businesses."

"I know."

But I really, really didn't want to talk to him. Not yet.

Krissa grabbed my hand. "It'll be okay, Rae. He's forgiven you, I promise. Do you want me to come with you?"

My eyes burned, probably from the rancid meat in my bag and not at all because the thought of hurting one of my other best friends made me want to curl up and cry.

"No, I want to talk to him alone. Will you take Bubbles home? I think he needs some rest."

"He needs some exercise," Krissa mumbled, but she held out

her arms and accepted the sleeping warplog. He didn't even flicker his eyelids. "You'll tell me how it goes?"

"Of course."

"I'll check on you later. Good luck."

"Thanks," I said. I needed it.

Krissa turned around, and I looked east down Main Street, where the sheriff's station was almost visible at the end of the street. Short rows of grass hugged the edge of the whitewashed exterior, barely hiding the sprouting mildew.

I hadn't been back since I'd rescued Valen, Hallow's Promise had split from Erline, and I told my longest friend that I'd picked to be with another man instead of him.

But I couldn't wait any longer.

I needed Leof's help.

Chapter 8

The building didn't collapse as I stepped inside, so Leof hadn't warded it to self-destruct with my presence. That was a good sign. I angled toward the hall that led to Leof's office.

"Excuse me, ma'am." A uniformed constable stood from behind the desk at the entryway. I froze and blinked, not quite understanding what I saw. Nobody had ever sat at that desk since I'd moved to Hallow's Promise. "What's your business at the station today?"

"I, um . . ." The little crease between my brows felt tight. "I work here?" It sounded like a question. If Leof had fired me, I hadn't been told, and Castor used me for his murder scene, so I probably still worked here.

The constable shuffled papers across the desk and finally picked up a worn parchment. "Name?"

"Uh, Rae."

He glanced at me. "Surnames?"

"It's just Rae. R-A-E."

"Ma'am, if you're not forthright about your identity, I can't let you into the building. I need to know your full name to check if you're on the approved employee list."

"Can you just look, please?"

His expression darkened, but he glanced at the page while he spoke this time. "There are new rules you must not be aware of, ma'am. Nobody unauthorized can enter the building unless they have an appointment and an approved employee escorts them for the duration of their visit. I'm willing to wager that you do not, in fact, have an . . ." His voice trailed off.

"Yes?" My voice was sickly sweet.

He flicked his gaze at me and squinted. Maybe he had poor eyesight. That explained his inability to find my name on the list.

"You are on the list. Just Rae."

"Thanks." I studied the badge on his chest. "Constable Drakemont."

He ducked his head. "Have a good day Miss . . . Rae."

I strolled past. A sort of sour expression tightened my throat. A lot had changed since the last time I'd entered the station. That made sense. Leof was the sheriff now, and securing the building would be one of his priorities. Positioning a guard at the main entrance was a small step in protecting his employees.

But it was *different*. Everything was different since I'd alerted the king to my location. And more changes would continue to unfold as we ventured deeper into the altercation with Erline. My heart raced. The fragile peace I'd enjoyed for over half a decade was slipping through my fingertips.

Leof's office sat in the heart of the station. I grabbed the knob firmly, a sarcastic comment about the new security guard primed on my tongue, and flung the door open.

"Leof, your—"

I sucked in a gasp.

The room was empty.

Well, almost empty. Leof's desk was gone, as were the

numerous awards and paintings previously adorning his walls. The fireplace across from the door was unlit and a chill that had little to do with the temperature crawled over my skin.

But two leather chairs remained perched in the center of the room.

Uninvited tears burned my eyes. I stepped into the room and closed the door quietly, so the neighboring offices didn't hear my intrusion.

Of course, Leof was gone. This was a marshal's office, and Leof was the sheriff now. He'd probably moved to the other side of the building and taken Jean's space. I hoped he'd destroyed the secret dungeons below that office—the ones where Valen had died.

I touched the top of one chair. Leof and I had spent countless hours in this room, sprawled across the chairs before the fireplace, discussing everything from casework to Suzie to gardening tips. Those discussions lead to case breakthroughs and put dangerous people off the streets. They fostered our friendship and allowed it to almost become something more.

And he'd left them here.

The tears leaked down my cheeks. I couldn't stop them. A horrible sob peeled from the bottom of my gut and clawed out my throat.

Leof had left these chairs here because I'd picked Valen. A clear sign he resented my decision and the fallout it provided to Hallow's Promise. If he couldn't stand to have these chairs in his new office, where did that leave me?

I let myself cry for a few minutes. I used to fear the emotion, any emotion, really. But Krissa cried all the time, and she reminded me that crying is only a reflection of being human. As the sobs tapered away and my eyes stopped burning, I swiped the liquid off my cheeks and stood straight.

Leof wasn't the only person in our friendship. If he wanted some space, I'd respect that, but I refused to allow our relationship to die without trying to keep it.

I left the empty office and walked down the hall to the other side of the station. The two sides of the building mirrored each other, exposing the same layout on both halves. The sheriff's office hugged the north wall and had exterior windows. Leof was moving up in the world.

The grand wooden door had space for a nameplate in the center, but it remained empty. Instead, the word "Sheriff" was scratched into the wood like a drunken wolf claw had gone rogue. Hopefully it was a good sign of Leof's claim of ownership and not a symbol of regret.

I tapped my fist against the door. As a werewolf, Leof had an incredible sense of smell, but I wagered the thick slab blocked most of my scent.

"Come in!" he called.

I did.

The room was big, way bigger than the office I'd just left. Leof's desk sat on the left side, and a small conference table with six chairs was on the right. He didn't have a fireplace, but there was a lovely painting of the exterior of the sheriff's station in the center of the wall. The whitewashed building looked better on canvas than in real life.

Leof looked up from the paperwork on his desk. I turned around so I didn't have to stare at his face while he realized who had invaded his office.

"Rae," he said. I analyzed his tone. He didn't sound mad or frustrated. He was slightly breathless, like I'd caught him off guard.

I turned and met his gaze full on, a smile on my lips.

"Hi, Leof."

The werewolf was handsome, I couldn't deny that. He had high cheekbones, a square jaw, and amber eyes that warmed me from the inside out. Muscles danced beneath his crisp uniform. I knew exactly how good he felt pressed against me. When he smiled, the whole world melted for a few moments.

I hadn't made him smile in a long time.

"Come here, sit down." He gestured to a chair from the other side of his desk. A chair that was not one of our armchairs.

Reluctantly, I sank into the unfamiliar seat. It was rigid and foreign against my back.

Leof crossed his arms and stared at me. I didn't have the right words in my mouth. They all felt heavy and angry.

Luckily, Leof spoke first. "I heard you're helping Castor with his case."

Oh, right. That's why I was here, not because of some silly chairs, but because someone had been murdered.

And also, sort of, because of the chairs.

"I went to the crime scene. There wasn't much left." There, perfectly normal words applicable to this conversation.

"Arson, right?"

"Seems like it."

"Did you find anything else?"

I'm guessing he didn't mean anything like a Provider trying to kill me. "Nope."

I shifted in the seat. There wasn't the usual flow of conversation between us. It came out stiff and cold, like Bubbles when he had to go potty in the snow.

Leof's gaze softened. He'd always been able to read me like a book. "Rae, how have you been?"

I jerked to my feet, suddenly too restrained by the unfamiliar chair in this strange room with the man I'd rejected but loved. The weight of everything tightened inside my chest and made it hard to breathe.

Leof stood too. I knew by the slide of his chair on the wooden floorboards. But he didn't come to me. Before . . . everything, he would have wrapped me in a hug. Now, I didn't know where we stood.

"You left the damn armchairs, Leof," I bit out.

"I . . . what?"

I spun back toward him and pointed one finger at his chest accusingly. "You left the chairs in your old office. You took a new title, a new office, and you *left the armchairs behind!*"

His brows somehow creased and raised at the same time. He studied me the same way I studied a bomb that might be ready to explode.

"I'm sorry?" he said. "If you don't want them, I can take them out."

"You should be." I poured more heat into my words, letting all the frustration and change mold into anger. "And you know what else—" His words sank through my thick skull. "Wait . . . what does that mean?"

Those golden flakes shimmered around his chocolate eyes, and for once, I didn't find them charming or delightful. No, they were downright annoying. He was laughing at me.

"I said, if you don't want the chairs, then I can arrange for them to be moved. It wouldn't be a problem. I'll have the table in here taken out."

The cogs inside my head turned, but they produced no thoughts. "What?"

He circled the desk, standing closer to me, and leaned one

hip against the edge. "That's why you're here, right? To move into your new office? Castor was supposed to tell you at the crime scene." He scratched the back of his neck. "I would have told you myself, but I didn't know if you'd be ready to see me yet."

The knot in my chest loosened while I tried to fit the pieces of the puzzle together.

"You're giving me your old office?" The question came out as a whisper.

"Castor didn't tell you. Damn it, I'd kill that man if I didn't need him." Leof stepped toward me. He smelled of spice and leather and an undertone of safety that I rarely got to experience. Every movement was slow, as though waiting to catch me when I tried to dart away. "I think you've earned a place to work that isn't the old broom closet. Besides, the caretaker is complaining about where to stash his supplies."

I giggled. "If you ask Castor, I've probably ridden them all far, far away."

"He's an idiot, but he's our senior constable and he'll grow into a great marshal. Or at least a good one. Honestly, a warm body in the job is all I can expect, but he checks that box. If you're not here about the office, what can I help you with, Rae?"

The list of shops felt heavy in my pocket. I did need his resources to help with this investigation.

But I needed Leof's friendship more.

I grabbed his hand. He tensed, staring at the contact.

"I'm sorry," I whispered. "I know that I've made a decision that hurts you, and there's no way to avoid that. I only hope that, with time, we can still be friends."

He squeezed my fingers and let go. "I'm always here for you. Even if I'm starting to question your piss-poor decision-making skills, I'm not going anywhere."

Leof was like the—my—armchairs. Warm, comfortable, dependable, solid. He was hurt, but he would be okay. We all would.

"I was going to ask for your help on my case," I admitted.

"Well, well, look how the tables have turned." We both laughed at the memories. A year ago, Leof had requested my help with a murder, and I promised it would be my last case. Turns out, I was a bad liar. "Tell me what you need."

"I have a list of places that buy and use sulfur, but I can't question all of them myself. I was hoping you could lend a few constables to do some interviews and see if anything suspicious comes up."

"Absolutely." He held his hand out, and I put the list of businesses into his palm. "You have access to all our resources now, except the ones in place for security and scouting. We must remain alert since I expect Erline to send soldiers any day."

"Thanks, Leof. Cross off the North Gate butcher's shop. I know the owner's daughter, so I'll talk to them personally."

"Got it. Anything else?"

An explosion sounded from outside, followed by a series of screams.

Leof launched from his seat, hands already shifting into wolfish nightmares.

I unsheathed my sword. More banging and the smell of smoke traveled down the hall.

"GIVE ME THE GIRL OR YOU WILL ALL DIE!"

"What the hell?" Leof murmured, heading for the door.

The weight in my chest turned to lead and sank all the way to my toes. I sighed and stared up at the ceiling for a handful of seconds. I'd heard bad things came in threes, except for me, where they came in hundreds.

"It's a Provider," I said. "And they're here for me."

Chapter 9

Leof and I rounded the corner to the front hallway as more screams erupted. My heart pounded while adrenaline poured through my body. When we passed the wall, a stream of blue and silver flashed in front of us—aiming at the poor constable that had questioned my arrival.

Constable Drakemont screamed, the sound abruptly cut. The beam sliced into his chest, absorbed as his eyes opened wide, but he never took another breath. The lightning pulse died as quickly as it came, and the man dropped to the ground with a scent eerily similar to cooked chicken.

A woman chuckled, smiling at her kill. She wore the typical Provider robe, the hood lowered across her shoulders. Shorter than me, with cropped hair and blue eyes that matched the lightning she'd just wielded.

I grabbed Leof and pulled him back around the corner before she aimed in our direction.

"Did she . . . did she just shoot lightning from her eyes?" he asked. No need to whisper while the rest of the station screamed and ran.

"Yes, I believe she did."

He sighed.

We dropped to our knees and edged around the corner, keeping our backs as close to the wall as possible. The Provider stared forward, caught for a moment while the magic built inside her body, and twin streaks of light snapped out of her eyes. Nobody screamed this time, so hopefully she'd missed.

"Do you have a plan?" Leof asked.

I glanced over my shoulder, in case someone else had arrived and I hadn't noticed, because he couldn't possibly be talking to me. Nope, the hallway behind us was empty.

"Me? I made the plan last time. It's definitely your turn."

The last time we'd worked together, I had led him and Krissa into a secret dungeon beneath the sheriff's station, found Valen, got him killed, and resurrected him from the dead. Toss in some murder and a splash of bloodshed and it had been a crap-salad.

Leof snorted. "You called that a plan? It was a series of bad ideas."

"It worked, didn't it?"

"If 'worked' means the king of Erline has made Hallow's Promise as his personal punching bag and sent his personal assassins into our walls, then yes, it worked brilliantly."

I blinked. He'd said 'assassins'—plural.

"You knew about the Providers?"

"I—" The werewolf froze. He locked his gaze forward, and his face turned red. Yep, I wasn't supposed to know that part. "Listen, we can talk later. Right now, there's a glorified storm cloud killing my constables."

According to Valen, he'd dispatched all the Providers that had entered Hallow's Promise so far—which meant Leof must have learned about them from Valen.

Valen had talked to Leof before me. I let the thought roll

around in my mind for a moment. Despite everything that happened, Leof and Valen were working together to protect Hallow's Promise.

And me.

"Right." I let that go—for now. "How about you run out there, and I'll stab her in the back."

"Great idea, except I like my skin attached to my body and not charred."

"That probably won't work, then."

"Why don't you cook her with some of your rediscovered death magic?"

"I . . . I can't right now."

Thankfully, he didn't press further. It would be embarrassing to admit that my necromancy only worked when I was emotionally pissed off.

"Then can't you do your science thing and deflect the lightning into her face or something?" He sort of fluttered one hand. "There's a mirror behind the desk, maybe that will work."

"No, the mirror will reflect the light of her bolts, which could temporarily blind her, but the actual strike would go straight through it. Unless you're volunteering to hold the giant target, that's not going to work."

The sound of words in a low tone carried from the other side of the hall. Judging by the muffled orders, some of Leof's people had created their own plan. Seconds later, a swarm of arrows lodged toward the Provider from the other side of the hall.

She *laughed*.

Sparks flew as the arrows that entered her personal space zapped out of existence in a blink. She had some kind of personal protective shield.

More arrows flew. Pale flashes highlighted Leof's face in baby blue as the Provider disintegrated every projectile. If it weren't such a terrible situation, it would have been a lovely color on the man.

I ground my teeth and studied the space. There wasn't much at the entryway of the office. The wooden desk along the front wall now contained cracks and splinters. A matching chair hadn't fared much better. The mirror Leof had offered hovered above the desk, proudly topping the fabric standard bearing the sheriff's star across the front.

I sat back on my heels. The wooden arrows couldn't handle the electrical charge as the interior water component vaporized immediately. They exploded. We needed a projectile that accepted her lightning.

Leof had asked for a science thing. Fine, I'd give him one.

"Can you get to the pole holding the standard in place?"

He peered around the corner. "Physically, yes. And remain in one piece? I'm not sure."

I rolled my eyes. "If I make sure you don't get zapped, can you get to the flag?"

"How are you going to do that?"

"I'm going to distract her."

"Again, how?"

"I thought I'd strip naked and start dancing, Leof."

He opened his mouth, but nothing came out.

If I kept rolling my eyes, they'd get stuck that way. "I'm going to distract the Provider, make sure you don't turn into holey cheese, and kill her. All you have to do is get me the flag."

"Fine, but I don't like it."

This didn't feel like the best moment to point out that he had never liked my plans.

The Provider had forced Leof's constables to retreat deeper down the hall. She smiled as she stepped out of the entryway and deeper into the station. Another blue flash and several shouts followed her path.

Hot anger boiled in my chest. I stood smoothly and pulled my sword from its sheath. Smoke coils curled up my arms, thicker and stronger than they had been while fighting in the field at Castor's crime scene. The magic felt slightly more familiar.

The Provider headed toward Leof's old office. *My* office. I wasn't about to stand here while she destroyed it before I'd even moved in. I started down the hall, planning to cut her off at the opposite side.

"Uh, Rae," Leof spoke softly behind him. "Your sword is smoking."

"Damn right it is," I said, and kept going. I was tired of hiding parts of me. They could take me as is, smoking sword and all.

I stepped into the center of the hallway, giving the Provider a clear view.

She blinked and squinted. I waited, my sword hanging at my side, smoke eagerly twisting along my ankles. She still didn't move. Maybe she had bad vision?

"Hello," I called. "It is I, the fabled necromancer the king has ordered you to recover."

She remained frozen. Hm, maybe she couldn't hear either?

I didn't know much sign language, but I'd caught a few phrases from my library-book-stealing days. They were thankfully over now, and I returned all the cherished library books I borrowed.

I awkwardly shuffled my sword to use both hands.

"I am the n-e-c-r-o-m-n-c-e-e-r," My fingers moved clumsily

with the word. "Sorry, I've never had to spell this out before, and I got a little lost. I think that's close, though."

She snarled. "What are you doing?"

"Oh, good, you do speak." I settled the blade in my palm. "So, you understand when I say that if you leave now, you can keep your life."

Her lips twisted into a sinister smile. "You are a little girl. You cannot be who the Highest seeks."

I held my hands out. "Sorry, but it is."

"You are very small."

"I'm taller than you."

She didn't like that. Blue danced in her eyes and trailed into her cheekbones. I hadn't noticed that from the other side of the hallway. Neat trick.

"I'll spare you the speech. The king of Erline wants me alive, but he didn't specify in good condition. You plan to torture me, confine me, or drag me back to Erline. I'm afraid I must adamantly oppose."

Her cheeks turned pink. Aww, it was so cute with all the blue.

The glow began in the blacks of her eyes, spread across the iris, and consumed the sphere completely. Uh oh, she'd decided she'd had enough of my taunting and jumped straight to the lightning part. Hopefully, she'd set her strikes to stun, or else Erline might receive a crispy necromancer.

I turned and ran back down the hall. Once the hair on the back of my neck rose, I flung my sword into the wall and dropped to the ground. The lightning followed the easiest pathway—thankfully, that was my metal sword protruding from the wall and not me. Well, that eliminated my backup plan of sword-versus-lightning combat, which was basically an immediate death sentence, anyway.

Smoke from her strike billowed heavily around the floor. My arms shook as I forced myself upright. When I turned, the Provider's eyes were already glowing again.

I glanced around. There was no cover and nothing else to take the brunt of her strike. If Leof didn't get the flag now, I would be the next body to smell like cooked chicken.

Sparks clawed their way around her eyeballs. I grimaced and held my hands up. It wasn't logic or fighting, it was pure instinct as though they could ward away the upcoming blow.

"Hey!" Leof yelled behind the Provider. She blinked, all that power still pooled in her gaze, but it was now turned toward the werewolf.

Leof fully stepped out of the corner. He held the flag in his right hand and the huge mirror from the entryway balanced across the front of his body.

I groaned. Had he not heard my explanation about why mirrors wouldn't work? The Provider didn't stop, her attention directed at my friend.

"Get away, Leof!"

He held his ground. I only saw the back of her head, but I knew the glow in her eyes peaked to deadly brightness.

Leof didn't move. He took aim and launched the flag over the Provider's head and straight toward me. I caught the standard in one hand as the Provider let her lightning launch.

I held my breath. I didn't want to watch Leof turn to flash fried meat, but I couldn't look away.

He threw the mirror and ran away—a mere moment before her bolt hit the glass.

I shook my head. What . . .

The Provider screamed. The mirror shattered, but she'd

gotten the full reflection of her strike right into her sensitive eyes.

Leof *had* been listening to me. Awww.

Without wasting the precious time he'd given me, I stripped the flag off the metal pole and shifted my new spear into a comfortable throwing position. I gripped my magic as hard as possible and forced the smoke behind me into submission. It groaned, thick and slow, but it moved.

Good enough.

I yelled and threw the pole like a haphazard javelin. My strength alone wasn't enough to persuade the blunt end to pierce flesh, but coils of my smoke pushed the projectile through the air. Magic drained from me, and I gasped. It hurt. The smoke kept the javelin up and increased its speed.

The Provider turned toward me. Her eyes were glowing, ready for another bolt.

It was too late.

She let her magic out as the metal struck her chest. Her lips spread into a circle, and the lightning caught the end of the pole, acting like, well, a lightning rod. The sparks rippled and flowed down the metal and her power spread straight into her chest.

My necromancy flared as her heart stopped instantly. It hovered around her death, tasting its sweetness. I allowed it a moment to relish, then drew it back in.

I collapsed on the floor. Sweat beaded on my forehead and dampened my shirt. Smoke-Wielding had taken all my magic and energy.

But the Provider was dead.

Leof's constables spilled from the rooms they'd sheltered in. They laughed in an awkward way that barely surviving death created, then circled me with thanks and gratitude. One man reached a hand out, but I waved him away. The floor was far more comfortable right now.

"Alright, everyone get away, leave the woman alone." The crowd parted and spat Leof out. "Someone get that body to the morgue—I need to send it back to Erline with a thank you note. And find Francis' next of kin. I have to notify them."

Francis must have been the constable who died at the front desk. My heart hurt, the only thing I had energy left to feel. He had died because of me.

Leof knelt beside me and put his hand on my shoulder. He must have read my mind because he said, "*They* all lived because of you."

Maybe.

I couldn't think anymore. Leof gently cradled me in his arms. There was a time when I would have rested my head on his chest and enjoyed his warmth against me. Today, I didn't. Not because I minded that he carried me. He was my friend, and I cared for him deeply. But because my heart was no longer conflicted.

I wished Valen were here. I wished he had picked me up from the floor and held me close. I didn't need any more time to process my past. I only wanted Valen in my future.

Leof set me on the ground before the fireplace in my new office and left. A moment later he returned, threw a blanket over me, and set my sword beside me. It faintly smelled of smoke.

"Brew just showed up outside," he said softly. "I'll stay until you decide to go home."

I had a hundred things to do, but instead, while Leof settled into the leather chair behind me, I closed my eyes.

Chapter 10

I didn't sleep long, maybe an hour or so, then I staggered out of Leof's—my—office and into my magic wagon.

Brew vibrated when I stepped inside. I sucked in a deep breath littered with the flavor of herbs, teas, and tonics. It was impossible to tell that a magical severed head hid at the back of the highest cupboard. I'd finally warded the entryways into the wagon, making it the perfect place to conceal the Oracle of Faedor. I didn't have to look at her to remember the head on its golden platter with her mouth open and tongue exposed. We were still searching for the magic rock to wake the Oracle from her slumber.

When I first started working at the sheriff's station, I didn't make enough money to survive. I turned my bad habit of stealing library books into a business selling teas and potions I learned from those books. Brew and I had established a reputation in town for crafting delicious and useful beverages.

Since the crime-solving business had improved, my reliance on selling drinks had decreased. But watching something I created have a positive impact on another person still brought immense joy to my days. It probably had something to do with my sheltered and traumatic childhood, but I wasn't about to unpack that.

The sun hovered above the horizon. Classes from the Central Campus of Mages and Magic would be getting out for the day. Meaning, a lot of desperate and sleep-deprived students would be eager for refreshing beverages.

I rubbed Brew's doorframe, and it warmed beneath my hand. "What do you think, Brew? Should we sell some tea?" The world was in chaos. Ignoring it for the rest of the afternoon couldn't make anything worse.

A jolt of joy ran through me. The wagon had absorbed some of my magic during our time together, and it had a sentience of its own. The king of Erline had banned sentient objects around the same time he started executing necromancers. Another charge to add to my list of crimes against the capital.

The world narrowed and stretched as Brew found the best ley-line route to get us close to the college. Technically, I wasn't allowed to sell on the campus grounds anymore. There was an incident that may have involved breaking into the dean's office and assaulting one of his pets. He never proved it was me, but he banned me on a very promising hunch.

Brew settled across the street from the campus. The cherry blossoms were budding on the light green branches. Students shuffled along like half-asleep zombies, their eyes focused on the ground before their feet. The bubbling of the pond fluttered in the distance, and the whole place smelled like fresh, crisp parchment.

I set the menu sign out front and straightened the BREW-TEA-FUL sign hanging beneath the ordering window. It didn't take long for the first customer to shuffle toward the wagon blindly, with her books sagging and expression resolved.

"One I'm-Not-Sleep-TEA, please."

Oof, she had dark circles beneath her eyes, and her voice sounded weak, tired. She needed an extra-strong drink. I gave her a warm smile, filled a kettle with water, and set it over the fire at the end of the countertop. The rear cupboard opened on its own, and I patted Brew's side in thanks while I pulled out my strongest tea. The bitter scent hit my nose. Hopefully, she really didn't want to sleep for quite a few hours.

As I waited for the water to bubble, I worked on peeling strips of an orange skin with a paring knife.

Tomorrow, I needed to talk to the North Gate butcher's shop about their sulfur purchasing and usage. I'd have to follow up with Leof on his constable's questioning, either in the evening or the next day. And another Provider attack could occur at any minute.

One of Brew's cupboards was magically spelled to remain cold, and I pulled it open and took out an egg. I cracked it into a glass bowl, dumped the shell on top, and whisked them all together into a crunchy froth.

More details about the case wandered through my thoughts, but my mind shifted to Valen.

He was the man I'd used to escape the capital. I'd taken the lives of five other people and poured them into Valen to turn him into a weapon. He'd slaughtered the guards defending the castle and granted me my freedom.

In return, I abandoned him in the rain and left him for dead.

But it turns out, that's not what happened. Valen had escaped Erline too—and taken some of my powers with him. He'd trained diligently to perfect that magic and helped Ilene build the rebellion from a dream into an actual army. He became the spy she needed to pass messages to other rebellion leaders and to find the missing necromancer that could turn the tides of war.

Me.

When Valen died last month, my world ended. I wanted to die too, just to lie beside him forever.

The water finally boiled. I dumped a generous amount of black tea into the pot. The water darkened immediately and released a sharp scent of tannins. Once the leaves floated along with the current, I poured the frothy egg into the pot, too.

Valen recognized me before I figured out who he was. He started training me with a sword so I wouldn't be helpless, and we'd moved on to working with my magic.

And I wanted him. I chose him, protected him, restored his life. I was tired of waiting to be with him because of some conversation. The moment he came back from this mission with Ilene, I was going to—

"I'm sorry." The customer outside leaned closer to the sash. The wards flashed a translucent red, but she didn't notice. "Did you just put an egg into my tea?"

I blinked and looked down. Cooked egg bits and pale shells flurried around the boiling water.

"Yes."

She jerked as though surprised. "Um . . . why?"

"Oh, sorry, I suppose that would look odd. This is a very bitter and strong tea, so the egg collects impurities and improves the flavor while it cooks. Don't worry, I'll filter out the pieces with the tea leaves so you won't taste any egg."

"That's a relief. I didn't know a nice way to say, 'No eggs in my tea, please.'"

We shared another chuckle. I poured some orange syrup into her mug, filtered the tea and egg mixture out, and topped it all with a splash of milk and a piece of orange rind. It smelled sweet and sharp and guaranteed a couple of good hours of studying.

"Thank you!" she called and handed me her coins. I dropped them into the box with a satisfying clang.

Brew's rear door jiggled.

I paused and squinted at the entrance. It jiggled again, and the wagon shifted uncomfortably. Someone was trying to get through the door, but Brew kept it locked.

I carefully stepped closer while the knob shook once more. I pressed my ear against the wood, and I swore Brew held its breath while I listened to the other side.

Silence.

I drew back and squinted at the door suspiciously.

A shadow jumped through the sash, my wards flashing red for a moment before fading away.

I. What? *No.*

Those wards were brand new. I'd had so many people jump into the wagon through the sash that I promised myself it would end. My own blood and a plethora of expensive herbs created the spell. The gods themselves shouldn't be able to get inside this wagon without my permission.

Anger burned hot through my chest. First, the king kept sending Providers to kidnap me, and they were making my warplog fat. Now, a stranger with a black face covering burst through my wards.

Not today, mister.

I pulled my sword. "I don't care who you are. You can either leave this wagon in one piece or multiple. It's your choice."

I took a step forward, but they moved faster. In a blink, they grabbed my sword hand, pushed me into the hard, wooden wall, and pinned my wrist beside my head.

The sword was still in my hand, but I couldn't move.

A grunt escaped my lips as I tried to punch with my other hand.

He caught that one, too.

Great. Both of my hands were incapacitated by a threatening stranger. If this was another Provider, I may have met my match.

Luckily, I still had both feet. I sucked in a breath and braced my knee to aim for the family jewels, right as my assailant pulled the covering off his face.

Valen.

The anger didn't fade. It fanned hotter and spread through my body. His magic reacted and cracked like ice along my skin.

"*You.*" That's why the wards didn't work. I'd created them to allow Valen and Krissa access as well. "I almost kneed you in the groin."

He gave me a half-smile. Damn it, my heart melted. No, I was trying to be angry.

"That would have been unfortunate," he whispered, and his breath caressed my face, fresh as spring rain and delicious as forest pine.

He hadn't let go of my wrists.

"I didn't think you'd be back yet," I said to fill the silence, to keep the man from hearing how quickly my heart pounded with each inhale of his scent.

"We were both eager to return." Valen shifted, gently pulling my sword from my grip and lowering it to the floor. He adjusted his grip to hold both of my wrists over my head in one of his hands. His other hand traced along my neck and tilted my chin up.

Oh my. His blue eyes burned as he studied my face.

"Hey, I'm trying to be mad at you," I said, but the anger was quickly transforming into another, equally intense feeling.

"You can keep trying." He bent down and pressed his lips to the side of my neck. The butterflies escaped my stomach and followed his touch. "Feel free to add some yelling, too."

Why did I think he'd like that?

I leaned my head back to give him more room. Valen groaned and pulled back.

I sucked in a breath and stiffened. He paused too, putting more space between us.

"What's wrong?" he asked.

"Don't you dare." A hardness clenched my throat, mixing anger and . . . fear. Fear of rejection.

"What?"

"Don't pull away from me. I can't handle losing you again."

Valen's brows creased, then smoothed. He laughed, a dark sound that curled at the very center of my body. He leaned in, stepping between my legs, forcing his body against mine. My eyes fluttered at just the smallest touch.

He put his lips against my ear. "You have all of me, Sunshine. I'm not going anywhere. Tell me what *you* want."

Everything.

"I want you, Valen." Was that really my voice? "All of you. Right now."

The mercenary smiled.

Then, his lips were on mine.

The world melted, or at least it felt that way. He tightened his grip beneath my chin and trapped me against him. Heat coursed beneath my skin and spread along every nerve. My head spun. I wanted to breathe, but didn't remember how, and it didn't matter, anyway. Valen was life and air and everything in between.

Our magic pulsed as fire and ice intertwined. It wound around us, mixing and separating, urging us to build it higher.

His tongue skirted my lips. I parted them, and his flavor overwhelmed me. The kiss changed, turning charged and frantic. Valen released my head and hands, moving to grip my hips, and hauled me against his body. He had me pinned against the wall, both of my legs wrapped tightly around his waist.

He felt so good. I never wanted to let him go.

But he broke away. Breathless, he looked at me as though I were the last sliver of light in a dark world, and he was lucky enough to behold it for the final time.

"Brew," he whispered, that cursed half smile tilting his lips, the desire deepening the pools of his eyes. "Take us home."

Chapter 11

Valen was in my bed.

That wasn't a surprise, of course. I'd been here when he crawled beside me, one arm carelessly across my waist like we'd slept this way a million times.

I'd also been on the couch when we'd ended up there.

And the dining table.

And the bed, but in a very different way.

I guess I should say: Valen was *sleeping* in my bed. And that felt . . . weird.

Good, really good. Right. It felt *right* that Valen was tucked in beside me and his soft breaths tickled the side of my face, moving my hair with each exhale.

Or maybe it felt like a dream. Because someone like me didn't deserve so much happiness. Or joy. Or love.

I gently ran my finger along his forehead, where the newly lengthened strands of hair brushed his skin. He was warm, and real, and here.

The wards pulsed.

Damn it. A gentle knock sounded against the front door, followed by a less than gentle knock.

Valen jolted upright, a knife gripped tight in one hand. Where did he even get that from? We weren't exactly clothed . . .

"Don't!" I jumped out of bed. "I'll get it!"

He eyed me, the look turning from sleepy surprise to sudden desire in a heartbeat. I . . . wasn't wearing any clothes.

Valen leaned back into the pillows and put both arms behind his head. "Like that?"

Despite everything that had happened tonight, a burning heat crawled into my cheeks. I didn't bother with a reply and grabbed a thick robe from on top of my dresser beside the bed.

"Bummer," Valen said as I tied the sash. "Why don't you let me get the door? Then we won't have to ruin such a pretty view."

I didn't know how to tell him that I would exchange the world to keep him in my bed. That if he got off the mattress, my heart might shatter into pieces. That this moment felt so fragile, even his weight shifting off the bed might end it all.

I smiled. "You can get the midnight visitor."

"You get a lot of those?"

He used to be one of them. "Unfortunately."

Habit allowed me to navigate the loft ladder in the dark, where the ember glows of the fire lit the first floor. More knocking followed by a few choice swear words allowed me to identify the visitor.

"Castor." I pulled the door open and let the anger burn in my eyes. "For what do I owe the pleasure?"

The constable, err, marshal, leaned back with a slightly wide-eyed expression. He wore casual clothing of black breeches and a white tunic, but his jacket was slung awkwardly across both arms. He shifted his gaze into the shadows, and I looked over his shoulder, too. The woods were dark, empty.

"We searched Toren's residence. It was full of illegal animal products . . . and this. I didn't know what else to do with it."

My brows creased. "Who's residence?"

"Toren. He's the burn victim."

"Okay, and what exactly did you find?"

He held out the bundle of fabric. "This."

Castor shifted again. He clearly felt uncomfortable carrying his cargo. I eyed it suspiciously. What sort of contraband did Toren smuggle that made an experienced officer so concerned?

I sighed. "You'd better come in."

He gave a harsh laugh. "No, thanks. I'm not falling for that again. Just take this and put it somewhere safe."

Not falling for what again? Oh . . . right. Last time I'd invited Castor into my house, I'd tricked him into crossing my wards. They'd been enchanted with a spell named Lightning-Crotch at the time. I wouldn't want to try that again either.

I held my hands out. Castor carefully set the bundle into my arms. His jacket draped around the sides of the object, leaving the bottom to brush against my skin. It felt rough, but smooth, like goosebumps on a cold night.

He waited, staring down.

Oh.

I pulled the fabric off and studied my new possession. It was

. . .

"An egg?" I asked.

It wasn't a normal egg. For one, it was huge. About the size of my largest mixing bowl. Also, the top and sides were sucked in, like the air was slowly deflating from the leathery shell. A large X was drawn on the top in black ink.

"We found it in Toren's fireplace. The coals had gone out, so it might not be viable anymore. I was hoping you'd know what it is, and how to care for it."

I ran my fingertips along the top of the egg and carefully reached out with my magic. A spark reacted to the touch.

"It's alive," I whispered. A sense of awe emitted from the item as I cradled it. The pure joy of new life forming in my hands. "This X is marking which side to keep the egg, so the embryo inside doesn't become crushed by its own weight. Unlike birds, reptiles don't rotate their eggs."

"Reptiles?" Castor ran a hand through his hair and glanced into the forest again. "You know what it is?"

I brushed the shell again. "It's a wyvern."

His nose crinkled. "Like a dragon?"

"They're more closely related to birds. Picture a snake with wings and feathers."

"I'd rather not. Do you think the mommy wyvern was responsible for the dead guy? If he was engaged in the illegal animal trade and stole her egg, she probably turned him into a crispy nugget in return."

I let the thought sit. "That doesn't explain the sulfur present at the scene."

"Wyverns don't emit sulfur as part of their natural accelerant, or whatever?"

"I don't know. I'd have to run some tests."

Castor leaned closer, careful not to cross the boundary of my wards. He grabbed my upper arm, and I tensed.

"Someone was following me on my way here," he whispered. "Keep it safe."

A flash of silver danced out of the corner of my eye. Valen smiled and perched a short silver knife against Castor's throat. The marshal stilled.

"Do not lay hands on her unless she asks," Valen said. His tone made my toes curl.

Castor retreated and nodded. Something had seriously spooked him if he didn't return Valen's threat. "The autopsy is tomorrow. If you can't attend, I'll send a summary."

"I'll be there," I said. Castor turned and left my porch, the wards prickling as he stepped off my property.

I turned to Valen, mouth open, but the words stuck inside my throat. He wasn't wearing . . . much. A pair of loose linen breeches slung along his hips, exposing all those lines of muscles I'd gotten to explore last night. My mouth went dry.

He smiled. "We'd better get that egg into the fire."

"I. What?" I glanced down. "Oh, yes, right."

The flames flickered when I approached the hearth. They adjusted to a low heat, glowing red and gold, the embers shifting to offer a small indent among the wood. I placed the egg into the makeshift nest.

"Do you think it will hatch?" Valen asked.

"It's still alive, so it has a chance. I can't say anything more than that."

We watched the egg for a few more minutes. It didn't do anything.

Valen touched the side of my waist. I jumped. I hadn't noticed his hand slip inside the opening of my robe. Actually, the sash was completely untied. When did that happen?

He kissed the side of my neck. "What do you want to do now?"

"Well, it's the middle of the night. I was hoping for some sleep."

"I'm not very tired anymore."

I leaned into his touch. The shivers turned into flames, filling me from the inside. "Maybe I am."

He ran his fingers through my hair and settled on a firm

handful of the strands. He pulled my head back into his shoulder, forest and rain making me dizzy, and relieved me of the rest of the robe.

"You just lean back and relax, Sunshine. I'll take care of you."

Oh, my.

Chapter 12

"You're glowing."

Krissa and Whiskers walked on my right, and Bubbles hopped along to the left. I looked down at my hands. Hm, there was a faint shine around my skin.

"That's just how I look in the sun."

Krissa shook her head, sending rainbow ribbons twirling about her face. "No, I've seen you in the sun, and you don't look like that. You're glowing because you and Valen finally did it."

"Did what?"

It took me a moment to realize Krissa had stopped on the side of the road. I followed, turning around to look at her.

She squinted at me. "Are you going to make me say it?"

I bit my lip. Gods, was I actually glowing? Because my face suddenly felt very hot.

"You had sex with Valen."

"Oh my gosh!" I spun away, which was an answer on its own. The warplog's eyes widened, probably because he secretly hoped I'd drop dead from embarrassment, and he'd finally get to eat me. "Why did you say it that loud?"

Krissa tugged my hand from my face and wrapped her arm

through mine. She pulled me along the cobblestones. "Tell me everything. How much ravishing was involved?"

"I will kill you. I'm very good at it now, and Bubbles will eat you, so nobody will ever find your body."

She eyed the warplog. "I'm not sure Bubbles wants to eat anything right now."

Okay, so I'd have to find another way to dispose of her remains. I'd figure it out.

She kept going. "I'm your best friend. And I know I haven't always been very supportive of Valen pursuing you, and frankly I do think that was a good judge of character on my part, but as your best friend, I'm obligated to hear all the juicy details."

I laughed, I couldn't help it. Krissa was my best friend, and the only one who remotely understood what it meant for me to be with Valen.

"It was . . . really nice."

She flung her free hand up. "Yes, every woman's dream—a really nice night. Please, stop with the specifics, or I'll have to clutch my pearls."

"You are impossible."

"I didn't always used to be like this. I learned it from you."

"That feels like an insult."

She winked at me.

Thankfully, the intersection near the North Gate appeared and ended the painful discussion. We turned onto Pledge Lane and headed east, where the North Gate butcher's shop appeared on the side of the road. It was a quaint little building, generally stocky and solid, built to survive anything the harsh weather threw at it.

I'd been planning to talk to the employees at the shop once I saw the location on Matilda's list of sulfur purchasers, but after last night's visit from Castor, I had more questions. Matilda's shop was in the heart of Hallow's Promise, perched along Main Street with the other popular stores. But the North Gate butcher's shop sat close to one of the two entrances into the city. Traveling hunters often looked for the closest place to cut and package their meat. Due to the proximity of the wild woods just beyond the city wall, the North Gate butcher saw more exotic animals and creatures than Matilda's place did.

If Toren had been involved in illegal animal trade, the shop might have information about odd animals appearing around town.

I stopped in front of the door and pointed a finger at Bubbles. "Behave in here. No begging for food."

The warplog burped in reply, which probably meant he would do whatever he wanted, like always.

The front door opened into a wide, mostly square room with a curtain separating the rear of the space. It smelled faintly metallic, but not overwhelming. Toward the front door was a white chair with detailed carvings along its sprawling mahogany legs. The chair was empty.

Footsteps tapped on the tile floor, and a young woman emerged from an adjacent side door. She paused when she saw us and squinted.

Mr. Haverhill owned the butcher's shop, and Celeste was his daughter. He was an old man that smelled faintly like aged milk, so Celeste managed most of the business. She was about my height, had blonde hair wrapped into a tight bun, and wore a blue dress with a white apron. Unlike Matilda, her apron was suspiciously devoid of blood.

She studied me. "You look familiar."

I hadn't expected Celeste to recognize me. We'd briefly

worked together last year.

"Rae." I held my hand out. She grasped my fingers. "You helped me with Magnolia Feron Galrod's murder last year."

"Yes, of course!" She did a little jump, which was very cute. "Tell me, whatever happened to the Nightingale? I'd grown rather fond of the creature and would like to hear that it's safe."

I glanced at Krissa. Whiskers stepped out from beneath her skirts. He lifted his pointed nose and gave a big sniff in Celeste's direction.

She pressed her fingers to her mouth. "Oh, is this him?"

"Yes, this is Whiskers." Krissa crouched and ran a hand over the hoglet's quills. "He's retired from the Nightingale business, though."

Celeste mimicked Krissa's pose and held her hand out. Whiskers glanced at Krissa before venturing to the other woman. He sniffed her fingers and carefully gave her a wet kiss. Gross.

"Aww, he remembers me." She stood. "I'm so glad you stopped by. I feel so much better knowing he's safe. Please, come in. How can I help you?"

I eyed the empty chair. "Your dad . . . ?"

Celeste rolled her eyes. "In the back chopping wood. I told him that I'd handle it, but he insists an old man ought to be good for something. Don't worry, he'll get tired soon and stagger inside looking for a drink. The man needs to lay off the ale, but I won't be the one telling him that."

Phew, that was a relief.

"We have a couple questions for a case, particularly about the shop's usage of sulfur. The Main Street butcher gave us a list of her clients that purchase sulfur, and your store was on it."

"Well, we don't directly use raw sulfur. Rather, when we burn it, the gases that are produced have a preservation effect. Essentially, if we're trying to make the meat last a little longer on the shelves, we might burn it over a sulfur flame. It smells awful, though. We don't do it very often."

"Have any of your supplies gone missing lately? Are your employees left unsupervised with it?"

Her eyes sparkled. "It's just me and my father here, so unless he's been rummaging through the stock bins, we're not missing any. And I guarantee he doesn't even know where the sulfur is stored. He's too busy thinking up the next thing to throw under his axe."

I smiled, but it didn't reflect the frustration inside. Clearly, Toren's killer didn't get his sulfur from here. Hm, maybe she'd have some leads about the egg brewing in my fireplace.

"Thanks, Celeste. That's very helpful. I do have one more question, if you have a moment?"

She smiled and gestured for me to continue.

"What do you know about wyverns?"

She blinked. "They're very rare. There's a rumor of a breeding pair outside the walls, but nothing is definitively recorded."

"Would you happen to know if they use sulfur as part of their ignitable breath?"

"I'm sorry, Rae. I have no idea."

"What about wyvern egg rearing? Or anything on the black-market animal trade?"

Her eyes darkened at that. "The trade is a terrible thing. All those creatures being confined in horrid conditions and getting sick or dying so someone can make a meager coin. If I knew anything about that, I'd be doing my best to try to stop it."

"But don't you, you know . . ." Krissa waved at the shop. "Chop up dead animals?"

"The animals that come into this shop have lived their lives out in the wild, as is intended. While it might not have been my first choice of a profession, this is the hand I've been dealt, and at least the animals processed here lived natural lives." A yell sounded from outside. Celeste tensed. "Sorry, I have to go check on my father."

She disappeared behind the curtain with a flash of sunlight. Krissa watched the fabric for a few seconds and turned to me.

"That was weird."

"What was weird?"

"That girl." She circled behind the desk. A stack of drawers pushed against the wall with little chalk labels across the front panels.

"Why do you think that?"

"She got all intense when you mentioned animal trades. Her eyes got spooky." Krissa wiggled her fingers in front of her own eyes to represent whatever 'spooky' meant. "It was pretty intense."

"She cares about animals. I don't think that's a bad thing." But Krissa pulled one of the drawers open and peeked inside. "Also, stop snooping."

"I'm not snooping. I'm investigating. Something that you're supposed to be doing."

"I don't need to investigate Celeste. She helped a lot when we were trying to find Whiskers."

"Yeah, that's another thing. Didn't she seem too invested in the Nightingale? Maybe suspiciously so."

"It's not suspicious. It means she was worried about him." I watched as Krissa pulled the next drawer open and peeked inside. Celeste had gotten heated about my questions. She already admitted that the butcher shop wasn't her dream job. Could she be secretly sabotaging black-market poachers? Maybe, but it didn't feel right.

Krissa gasped.

Fine, I broke and stepped closer to Krissa to peer into the drawer.

"It's empty," I said. "I told you that Celeste isn't involved in this."

"Rae, that's exactly the problem." She pushed the drawer closed. Neat, white letters with a little swirl along the bottom spelled the word *SULFUR*.

I tried to put some logical explanation to the empty space. "That doesn't make sense. Celeste said they don't use the sulfur very often and nothing was missing from their supplies."

"Yeah." Krissa gave a harsh laugh. "Because it's already gone. Probably from lighting a certain illegal tradesman on fire."

A door creaked. I jumped, and Krissa slammed the drawer closed. We both faked smiles when Celeste emerged from behind the curtain.

"Sorry about that. Father still has both hands—for now." She rolled her eyes. "Is there anything else I can help you with?"

I wanted to ask about the sulfur. Krissa must have seen it on my face, and she shoved her elbow deep into my side.

"Ouch!" I said, but she was already talking over my outburst.

"Have you ever seen one—a wyvern?" Krissa asked. I rubbed the new sore spot on my side.

"Yes, once." Celeste's voice sounded similar to mine last night, while I cradled the egg in my arms and felt the life brewing inside.

"Did you process it?" Krissa asked.

Celeste shivered. "Oh, no. It was very much alive. I was walking home late one night and decided to take a shortcut. Bad idea, I know, but it wasn't the first time I'd gone that route. It seemed safe enough. Only a few steps off the road, I felt something watching me in the woods. I ran, and it chased me. Once the forest finally spat me out, I turned, and the wyvern was right there. For whatever reason, it had let me go."

Krissa leaned in. "You were walking home? This happened *here*, in Hallow's Promise?"

"Oh, yes."

"Where?" I asked, but I knew what Celeste would say. Only one strip of forest inside the city walls harbored monsters straight out of nightmares.

"The Void."

Chapter 13

Valen, Leof, Krissa, and I huddled inside Brew at the edge of The Void. Krissa's smile made me a little uneasy.

"Look at us, all huddled together in this much-too-small wagon and considering embarking on a dangerous mission. It's just like old times."

Apparently Bubbles agreed because he burped from inside his cupboard, which once held my brewing kettles and now cradled a plush blanket just for the warplog. Whiskers had stayed home with Ilene, who apparently had rebellion business to work on.

"We're not 'considering.' We're making a strategic plan."

Krissa and Valen made eye contact over my head. She rolled her eyes.

"I know what you're thinking, and contrary to popular belief, I am capable of making good plans."

"Of course you are." Leof leaned one hip against the countertop, which also put a little space between him and Valen. The two men had shared a few looks in the short time we'd crammed inside the wagon, but I was ignoring them. In fact, that was a perfect example of one of my plans. I planned to ignore them both all night.

"Why, exactly, are we hunting a dragon?" Valen asked.

"It's a wyvern, and I'm glad you asked. Someone or something turned Toren into a piece of coal. I tested the surrounding trees from the crime scene that also had burn damage and discovered sulfur was used in the arson process."

"I already have twenty constables asking local businesses about the sulfur, Rae," Leof said.

"And I appreciate that. However, Castor discovered a wyvern egg at the victim's house, and apparently other evidence of animal trafficking. He's wondering if the mother wyvern might have targeted Toren for stealing her egg, and I honestly don't know the answer to that."

Leof crossed his arms. "Are you planning on asking her?"

"Not exactly, and that's where you come in. My contact says she saw a live wyvern in Hallow's Promise once."

"Let me guess." Valen gave me a half-smile. "In The Void?"

"Yes! And—here's the part you've been waiting for—I'm planning to persuade the wyvern to breathe fire so I can collect a sample of its natural accelerant for comparison."

It was silent for three seconds.

"Persuade?" Valen asked. "You mean piss off?"

"I was thinking more like 'gently antagonize.'"

Leof pinched the bridge of his nose. "That's not a plan. It's a suicide mission."

"Only if we die. Which we probably won't."

"*Probably?*" Krissa repeated.

Alright, clearly, I was losing them.

"Listen, I will do the gentle antagonizing. While I'm busy with that, I need you guys to scrape some burnt bark off the trees. Then we can all go home."

"What's left of us," Krissa murmured. I sent her a sharp look.

Leof crossed his arms. "You brought me all the way out here to peel bark off a tree?"

"Not exactly. The wyvern isn't the only thing that lives in The Void. I want you to hold off all the other creepy-crawlies, so they don't kill us."

"Yeah, I don't want to be killed by anything other than the dragon," Krissa said.

"It's a wyvern."

"I don't know the difference."

"They're smaller."

"Oh, thank you, that's so much better. I don't want to be killed by anything other than the *smaller* dragon."

I took a deep breath. Valen touched my shoulder. His touch centered me, until I looked at his face. He was laughing.

My anger became hot, quick. "Next time we need a plan, don't look at me. I'm retiring from the planning business."

"Can't call it much of a business," Krissa whispered.

I grabbed the coin box from the top of the sash. Brew threw the rear door open, apparently anticipating my sour mood. I didn't even pat the wagon in thanks, which made me even more grumpy.

"Where's she going?" someone asked, but I was already lost in the darkness of The Void. Me and my coins versus an antagonized wyvern. Compared to the company I'd just abandoned, it sounded like a great time.

* * *

Everyone else had followed me. Apparently leaving me alone

in the enchanted woods didn't sound like a great idea to Valen or Leof, and Krissa refused to be alone.

I'd stacked the admittedly meager pile of coins in the center of a small clearing. Similar to their dragon kin, wyverns enjoyed gems, gold, and anything that sparkled. I had shockingly few of the first two, but I'd also tossed in some freshly polished used pots that I hoped scratched that shiny itch.

No luck so far.

I sprawled on my stomach facing the bait, both hands clasped under my chin. Krissa laid her head on the backs of my knees. I couldn't see Leof or Valen, but assumed they'd made themselves comfortable as well.

"Don't you think we should look into Celeste before risking our lives in The Void?" Krissa asked. She sounded tired.

I sighed. "I really don't think Celeste is involved."

"Who's Celeste?" Leof asked.

Krissa didn't bother lifting her head. "Her father owns the North Gate butcher shop. We asked her about the store's sulfur supply this morning, and she claimed they rarely used it. But the supply stock was completely empty. And she hates animal traffickers. I think fire-bombing Toren used up all their sulfur."

A few tense moments of silence passed.

"You mean to say," Leof's voice was hard. "You have a perfectly good suspect with some solid circumstantial evidence and instead of questioning or investigating her, we're all out in the woods searching for a dragon?"

I pinched my fingers together. "Wyvern. Smaller."

Even though I couldn't see the werewolf, I knew his face was pinched and red.

"Rae, this is ridiculous. I'm going home. Suzie's supposed to get back tonight or tomorrow, and I'd rather wait for her than sit one more minute staring at a pile of pots and coins."

Branches cracked as Leof stepped forward. The timing wasn't quite right though. His feet hit the ground moments before the twigs snapped. I froze and held my breath. The wolf kept moving, but he was used to the forest floor and stalking his prey in absolute silence. He didn't break a single twig.

More snaps.

I sucked in a breath and Leof halted. His eyes flashed amber as he searched the shadows.

A musty scent escaped from the depths. It felt a little moist in my nose, not at all like the sharp smoke I'd expect from a fire-breathing creature. Seconds later, something white and flakey streamed over our heads. It impacted against the adjacent tree in a big splat with ribbons of pale pearls expanding outward.

Krissa jerked upright. "Uh, what was that?"

I rose to my knees and studied the mystery substance. The tendrils caught tight against the bark, almost clinging to the rough edges. The wispiness and cotton-like strands looked familiar.

Leof slowly stepped forward and stuck his hand in the mess. It hugged his fingers, strong and firm.

"It's a . . . web?" He glanced back at me, brows raised.

"There's only one creature large enough to produce a web that big," I said. My heart rate picked up, a sudden ocean roaring in my ears. "Its common name is the House Spider."

"Aww," Krissa said. "It doesn't sound bad. Maybe even sort of cute, in a weird way."

I shook my head because it wasn't cute at all. "It's called that because it's the size of a house."

Everyone paused. More snaps filled the air, and I pinpointed the sound from above us.

Krissa pinched her eyes closed. "Please, please tell me there's not a spider the size of a house above me."

I followed the trees up and up, where the leaves met the dark sky and moonlight refused to enter the canopy of The Void.

Vivid red eyes blinked in the darkness—eight of them.

Chapter 14

"RUN!" I screamed.

The pitter-patter of steps echoed overhead. Moonlight illuminated a shadow that aimed straight for the space I'd occupied moments ago. The House Spider released a piercing screech and scampered over to the next tree.

We ran. I hated running. It usually meant I was fleeing for my life, and a single misstep could be my last. My sides burned and my lungs complained, but the giant spider stalking us from above was great motivation to move faster.

Krissa sagged behind. She didn't have regular cardio training as part of her swordsmanship practice sessions. Her eyes met mine as her toes caught on a root and she tumbled.

Damn it.

I pulled up short and grabbed her elbow. Her fingers shook as she gripped my hand and rose to her feet.

"You're okay," I assured her, random words falling from my lips, speaking out of pure panic. "We're all going to be okay."

Krissa nodded, and we surged forward. A wad of webs licked our heels. We'd been moments away from becoming spider chow.

Matching Krissa's pace kept us at the back of our group. Leof glanced behind, and judging by his wide gaze, we hadn't made much progress at outrunning the spider.

Valen fell into step beside me.

"Now would be an excellent time to use your magic, Sunshine."

I don't know how he kept his tone level as he ran. I gasped for breath, and a lingering pause followed every word.

"What? I. Can't. Do. That. It. Would. Kill. The. Spider."

"That's sort of the point."

I shook my head. "I can't kill it."

Valen looked at me, then glanced over his shoulder. "I'm not sure it's having the same hesitations."

"Listen, the House Spider is just doing what House Spiders do. I can't kill a perfectly innocent creature because of its nature!"

"I don't know why I'm surprised. First the warplog, then the Nightingale, but it's rescuing the giant spider that caught me off guard. Why do you keep collecting creatures that want to eat you?"

"Hey!" Krissa sucked in more air. "Whiskers hasn't tried to eat anyone!"

"She's got a point," I said. "Also, I collected you, and you haven't eaten me at all."

Valen sent me a smoldering look that made my cheeks turn pink. This was certainly not the time for the warm, tingly feeling in my stomach.

"What about Leof?" Krissa shouted. "Didn't you bring him specifically to avoid these kinds of confrontations?"

The wolf didn't look back again. "Do you think my claws can do any damage to that thing? It would thank me for the lovely massage before biting my head off."

"Okay, you then." Krissa turned on Valen. "We could really use some magic smoke right now. Maybe the kind that can trip giant spiders?"

Valen raised his brows and glanced at me. I bit my lip. "I don't think even Valen's smoke can hold something this massive. If we can make it to the clearing, Brew can take us out of here."

"As long as the spider doesn't hitch a ride with us," Valen said. "Do you think the wards on your cottage can fend off a primordial being the size of a house?"

I grimaced, or whatever the equivalent expression was, while frantically panting. "Let's get to the wagon first so we don't have to find out."

But Krissa and I were definitely slowing. Valen glanced at me with an expression that almost certainly said, *Either kill the spider or ditch the slowpoke,'* to which I responded with a scowl that meant, *'Go screw yourself.'* Glad to know our evolving relationship still included insults.

A pile of moist web launched into our path. Krissa screamed, and I grabbed her arm, jerking us to a halt. The four of us stared at the blockage for a precious few seconds. Leaves showered us, and wood groaned as the spider scurried overhead, hidden in the shadows.

"We have to go another way!" Valen peeled off our route and angled into the trees.

I hesitated. Brew was so close, right beyond the next line of trees. Running through The Void was a great way to get lost and disappear forever.

Krissa screamed. One hairy leg crawled out of the tree overhead, followed by another. They were massive, consuming almost half the tree as it staggered toward the ground. Its head lifted, an intensity of pure instinct lighting its eyes.

Yep, it definitely wanted to eat us.

Krissa grabbed me this time with a silent scream caught on her lips. Together, we followed Valen's trail deeper into the forest.

The House Spider pursued.

"We need to do something!" Krissa shouted. "It's going to enjoy a relaxing meal once we all collapse from exhaustion."

Everyone glanced at me. I shook my head. "Oh, no. I am not making a plan after how you treated me earlier."

"What if." Krissa gasped. "We all apologize very nicely?"

Valen looked at Leof. "There's a clearing up ahead." I don't know how he knew the layout of The Void. "Can you distract the spider long enough for me to get there first?"

Leof raised his hands, which were ragged mixtures of palms and claws. "Do these look like they're any match for *that*?"

Another wad of web smacked the ground in front of us. We lurched around it. My chest burned, and each breath stabbed a knife deeper into my side. Krissa was right. It was mere minutes before I became spider food.

"I can do it," I said.

If I thought it were possible, I would say Valen almost stumbled. Almost.

"You're going to kill the spider? With magic?" he asked.

"No, I . . . can't explain it, Valen, but I don't want to hurt innocent things with my power. The sheriff, the Providers—they hurt people. This spider just wants to survive." A pounding sound rang in my ears. "But I can distract it long enough to buy you some time."

The mercenary stared at me, or at least he tried to while we ran through the forest. He gave me a swift nod.

"I'm ready when you are."

Normally, I used my breath as a focal point to draw on my magic. That would have worked this time, except I didn't have any air in my lungs, and a hot poker was trying to stab down my throat.

I embraced the pain. I let Krissa's touch on my elbow guide me through the woods in blind trust, and I pulled my magic from the depths. It swelled up, sluggish and slow, but responsive. Tendrils of necromancy spilled around us.

Life and death whispered to me. Something had died long ago among the rotten logs beside the river. Sparks of life billowed in the creek, along the leaves, bedded down in cozy nests. They all called to me. My magic caressed each lifeless body—big and small—and sucked off the remnants of power clinging to the bones. The flickering lives whispered sweet nothings in my ear.

So much promise, it said, *so much power.*

It was right. Taking the lives of everything inside this forest would give me the ability to raise the dead several times over. I wasn't sure I could manage that, not because of any lack of power, but because I didn't want to.

These lives, I told my power, *they are good. They belong here. I don't want to take them.*

The magic softened. *You belong here, too.*

It faded, not completely, but enough that I stopped drowning in it. I gathered the remaining pieces and aimed them at the giant spider.

Its life pulsed brighter and heavier than the other creatures I'd touched tonight. Parts of it ebbed and flowed into the forest, the trees, the very air around it. The Void must provide some of its magic to the inhabitants. In return, it received protection from the civilization around its borders.

A symbiotic relationship.

I mentally sent my magic toward those places where the spider's magic tied it into The Void. As long as the House Spider drew power from the forest, we'd never outlast it.

Compared to my power, these hinge points were weak and crumbling. My magic overpowered the connections and snapped them apart. One by one, the spider lost its attachments to the forest.

But I hadn't accounted for those severed bonds longing for reattachment. They screamed inside my head. The separation was too fast and sudden. The spider couldn't maintain its life force with such a definite divide from its power supply.

It was alone.

I stopped running. The pain and longing were too much. They flooded my mind and smothered any other thoughts beyond *need*.

The spider stumbled. It missed the next branch and toppled out of the treetops. It landed on its feet, unharmed but dazed, and blinked its beady eyes at us.

At me.

It was dying. My power relished in the pure magic of death. But I didn't. A stab of guilt cut into me. I'd been trying to preserve its life and had stolen it instead.

I reached my hand out. "I'm sorry," I whispered.

The broken connections cried. In my mind, they surrounded the spider like hollow arteries, oozing its life out one pulse at a time.

A tendril of my power cradled one of the arteries. It wrapped around the wound and covered it, pulsing magic back into the spider through the new point of contact.

Death eased away.

I gasped. I'd severed the connection to the forest too quickly, but that wasn't the only available source of power—I was one, too. I could reconnect and supply the spider with my own magic.

My power picked up the broken bonds and reattached them—to me. The influx of this strange life connected to my own ramped up my necromancy. It sang a song only in my ears, one of life and rebirth and death and the beautiful tapestry they wove together.

The spider straightened. It stepped toward me, but I did not back away. I lifted my hand as it neared, closer and closer, and pressed its hairy, wagon-sized head against my palm.

Because it was mine.

Chapter 15

Dark smoke overwhelmed us. It brushed against me and the House Spider and blocked Krissa and Leof from our view. The tendrils were ice against my exposed skin, and they tickled happily along my neck. Chills dipped down my spine.

"Sunshine." Valen emerged from his smoke. "You continue to amaze me."

"I . . ." I looked at the spider as it quivered in front of me. It was . . . happy. As happy as an eight-legged bug-eating creature could be. "I don't understand what happened."

"What happened is that I had a perfectly good plan, and you decided to mess everything up by Captivating the spider." He brushed his hand over the creature's hairy abdomen. The spider curled in response, as enamored with Valen's touch as I was.

"Captivating?" I asked.

He studied me. "Haven't you done much research into your own type of power, Rae? Into your necromancy?"

Uh oh—he'd used my real name.

"No. I didn't want to do anything that risked my location. Asking for books on banned magic is a good way for a Provider to show up unannounced."

"Captivation is a rare talent among necromancers. It's the ability to take a life and bind it to your own, temporarily overwhelming their will."

I flinched. "That's awful."

"Is it?" He gestured to the creature. "Does the spider think it's awful?"

No. Only pulses of joy emitted from the spider.

"You have choices, Sunshine, just like the rest of us. You could make this connection painful and tortuous. But you've decided you want the spider to be happy. You can sever the bond at any time, and it will return to doing things that House Spiders do. I'd prefer you wait until we're out of eating range, though."

"Can you do this?" I asked.

His eyes soften. "No, Sunshine. I only have the tiniest bit of your power. Life and death are solely in your hands."

My throat closed. I didn't ask for this cruel ability—to steal another being's will. "Can this happen to people, too?"

Valen shrugged. "Probably, but I imagine Captivating a person is much harder than a big bug." He stepped closer. The icy touch of his smoke gave way to the brush of his hands on mine. Valen wrapped his arms around my waist and drew me close. His scent covered the mossy smell of the forest.

He tucked his finger under my chin and forced my eyes to meet his. There wasn't any fear in his gaze—just heat.

"You are the most amazing person in the world." He leaned down and brushed a kiss on the corner of my lips. "You never cease to amaze me." He kissed the other corner, wove his fingers into my hair, and tilted my head back to give access to my neck. He kissed me there, too. "I am in awe of you, Sunshine."

I could force creatures to do my will.

"I'm a nightmare," I whispered. "A monster."

"Maybe." He slid his hand up my neck to grasp my jaw and pull me closer. "But you're my monster."

Valen leaned down to kiss me, heat and ice, smoke and spiders, and every other kind of nightmare as promises between us. But he didn't care. He saw *me*, and he wanted me.

Our lips touched, rough and needy. I parted for him, enjoying his flavor, the way his lips tasted slightly of smoke. He growled against my mouth. I smiled in reply, earning a gentle nip.

An ear-splitting roar emitted through the trees.

Valen paused. Somewhere, someone screamed.

I pulled from his grasp as Valen sent his smoke away. The forest cleared in a moment. Krissa screamed again. Valen and I lunged forward with the large spider in our wake. I didn't tell it to move, but it followed like a lost pet.

I ducked around a tree and barreled into an incredibly hard object—one that yelled and tumbled toward the ground. Krissa clutched my arm as she fell, bringing me down with her. Hard ground met my stomach, stealing what minimal breath I had left.

I had thought the House Spider was horrifying, but the thing in front of us was a nightmare mix of a snake, a bat, and a bird. It had a narrow torso that cradled leathery wings tucked into each side. Rows of downy-looking feathers in vibrant shades of green and gold lined the creature's back. Overall, the creature was about the size and height of Brew, except for a long tail wrapping around the back of its scaled body.

A clawed foot twisted in front of me. Hm, the foot appeared disproportionately small compared to the rest of the creature. Funny that when death stared at me, I started comparing body ratios.

Krissa struggled onto her elbows and flipped to her back. She studied the beast in front of us the way I would study one of her mathematics books. Uninterested and slightly nauseated.

She pointed to it. "You said they were smaller."

"I said they were smaller than dragons—not that they were *small.*"

Her eyes narrowed. "That is specific to the point of being unhelpful."

"Have you ever seen a dragon? Trust me, this is smaller."

The wyvern blinked vivid flame-colored eyes as we finished our conversation. Apparently, he wasn't content with the outcome because he grumbled and released a wave of hot air that tried to blister my skin. It noticed the enormous arachnid behind us and shifted its gaze.

Leof also looked at the spider. "Do I have to choose which one eats me for dinner?"

"Ignore the spider," I said.

"Right, I'll ignore the giant, flesh-eating spider. No problem."

I rolled my eyes. "The spider is mine now. I'll explain later, but he's not a threat."

The wyvern swirled one golden eye on us and sucked in a breath. Valen grabbed my elbow and pulled me up. Krissa followed.

"Duck!"

The fire escaped over the tops of our heads. Intense burning seared the edges of my nerves. Krissa cried out.

"Can you do the thing you did to the spider to the dragon?" Valen asked.

"It's not a—oh, never mind. I can try."

I pinched my eyes shut and reached out to the spider attached to my power. It was so vibrant and easy to reach. It longed for the contact. It didn't want to be alone.

I aimed that magic toward the wyvern. Lines of power immediately lit its body in my mind. The place where flesh and magic created life, all the locations where strikes would wound or kill the beast.

Nothing connected the wyvern to the forest. It didn't have any outside bonds for me to overtake. It craved nothing.

"Nope," I said. "It would be very happy to kill us."

Another blast of flame aimed our way. We screamed and scattered.

"Rae!" Krissa pointed.

A shimmering flame danced between the trees. Brew! The wagon had found another ley-line through The Void.

We all sprinted toward the wagon. The wyvern released another stream of fire, which licked our heels—and not in a good way. The rear door of the wagon flew open, and everyone piled inside.

Except me.

Valen turned around. His eyes grew dark.

"Sunshine, get in."

I pressed my lips together. The House Spider and I were connected. I couldn't leave it to die.

And I needed a sample of the wyvern accelerant.

"Brew, take them home."

The mercenary headed toward the door. Rage burned in his eyes. "Rae, I swear, if you—"

The wagon's door slammed shut. A heartbeat later, it disappeared, taking my friends safely with it.

Leaving me alone in The Void with a Captivated House Spider and a very antagonized wyvern.

Chapter 16

My sword started smoking. It either fed on my fear or realized that the wyvern could swallow it in one gulp. Either way, smoke spilled at my feet and lingered along the forest floor.

The wyvern half-slithered, and half-strolled—more of a glide, really. Its vivid eyes pierced me, threatening fire and flames.

"I don't suppose you'd care for a cup of tea?" I asked. "I promise it tastes better than me."

The beast opened its mouth, exposing a flicker of flames in its throat. I swallowed a gulp and ducked to the side. Streams of flames and heat devoured the space I had just vacated.

Hm, death by wyvern fire hadn't been on my to-do list, but I had plenty of trees to collect a sample from now.

The House Spider flickered into view. It screeched at the wyvern and launched an attack, both front legs lifted high. The reptile hissed in reply, and the two engaged in an exchange of hair and scales I could barely track.

I used the distraction and ran to the nearest tree. The smoking bark burned my hand, but I peeled it from the tree, anyway. Adrenaline washed away the pain. I'd feel it later.

With charred bark filling my pockets, I drew my sword from its sheath. Gray, misty arms fell from the blade. It buzzed in my hand, warming the new blisters forming from the burns.

I ground my teeth and focused on the smoke. Controlling the wispy arms felt a lot like trying to catch sunlight. It looked pretty, but fell from my grasp with the slightest touch. I concentrated, trying to channel the same magic I'd used to Captivate the spider. The smoke was different, though. It was lighter, more air than power, and it had a mind of its own.

My jaw hurt. If I kept clamping my teeth together, they were going to get stuck that way.

The smoke slowly pooled and spread across the forest floor. The wyvern sent another spray of flames in my direction, but the spider's well-timed webs smothered them instantly.

My faint, misty tendrils crawled up the wyvern's body. They weren't nearly strong enough to trap such a powerful beast, but I didn't need to stop him. I needed to blind him.

The creature thrashed between the thickening smoke and the spider's assault. It screeched and launched more fire. My smoke slowly filled the battleground. Valen was able to smother light in a heartbeat. It took me several minutes before the mist finally concealed the wyvern completely.

Sweat pooled on my forehead and soaked the back of my tunic. My lungs hurt as I heaved in more and more air. It wasn't enough. I'd burned through my meager power after Captivating the spider and the smoke ate up my remnants. If the wyvern found its way out of the fog, I would be dead.

I ran. Well, staggered, really. I weaved around trees, and admittedly smacked into a few, heading toward the road. The strands of magic connecting me to the House Spider tugged as I ran and it followed. It covered my retreat, keeping the wyvern far behind.

The trees ended. I spilled onto the cobbled street and fell to my knees. My hands shook and my vision swam.

A shadow danced through the trees. The spider's glowing red eyes watched me around the trunks. I felt its sharp hesitation. The Void was its home—it didn't care to leave.

I shakily rose to my feet. "Thank you," I told the monster in the darkness. "Thank you for everything."

It blinked. An emotion akin to confusion ran through our bond, but it recognized my appreciation.

I let it go. My magic wanted to keep the spider. Afterall, a giant beast at my service might be beneficial. And that was where I drew the line. I didn't want servants. One by one, I severed the places our magic connected and reforged its bond to the forest. When the last tie snapped, the spider blinked twice, hissed, and scurried away.

It was done. I had the wyvern fire samples. We'd all survived. Someone clapped behind me.

I lifted my sword into middle-guard but knew I moved too slow. If the intruder wanted to kill me, I left my back exposed.

Valen stepped into the light cast by an oil lantern. I lowered my sword, but the look on his face was jagged and dangerous. His magic licked my skin, savored it, and burned angrily.

He stepped closer. I hesitated, taking half a step back. A twisted smile crossed his face, and he kept coming. He stalked me in the dark, and he liked it.

I turned to . . . run? And he grabbed my arm, pulling me close.

"You made me leave you," he whispered. A sharp edge lined his words. Silver flashed in his eyes. He squeezed my hand hard enough that I dropped the sword. My own anger rose to match, but a different kind of heat built in my body.

Oh, gods. I was gone. This man owned me completely.

"I was trying to keep everyone safe."

"Shhh." He pressed a finger against my lips. "You made me leave, Sunshine. And I'm so *tired* of leaving you. I had to walk away over and over again for the past year. I told myself it was better that way. You deserved to know the whole truth before anything happened between us." His gaze roamed my face, and lower, coming back to rest where his fingertip touched my lips. "Now, there's nothing keeping me from you. If you want to handle something on your own, just ask. You don't need anyone's protection. But if you *force* me away from you again . . ."

A wave of ice slipped through my clothing, both chilling me to the bone and trying to burn me from the inside out. I gasped, my body at war with itself.

If I asked, Valen would stop. He'd let me go and give me space to sort myself out.

I didn't ask.

"There will be consequences," he finished.

I jerked my chin up. "Like what?" I asked around his finger.

His lips pulled into a wicked smile. "The kind where I have to tie you up and make sure you can never leave me again."

Oh, *my*.

I leaned into him. His heart pounded against my chest, so real, so alive. I sucked in a deep breath until my lungs wanted to explode.

"Is that a promise?" I whispered.

He pulled me close, his lips pressed against my neck. There was a tremor in his touch, though. The way he held me, as though I were precious and fragile and he needed to cradle me. I had frightened him.

I wrapped my arms around his waist. Blisters ached across

my palms, and I needed a healing potion for all my wounds. They all paled in comparison to this moment.

His ear brushed my cheek, and I turned my head.

"I love you," I whispered.

He stilled.

For a heartbeat, a sudden pulse of doubt cut through my heart. Maybe it had been too soon. We'd barely figured out what this life might hold for us.

Then, he drew back to look at me.

His voice was raw, rough. "I am consumed by you. With you, I am at my weakest and my strongest, and there is nothing in this world that comes close to the ache inside my soul that only your company eases."

I laughed. I couldn't help it. "Who knew the Nightwrath had such a way with words? Don't let your friends hear you talk like that—they might kick you out of the rebellion."

"You know what?" Flames danced in his eyes. "I also hate you."

But he pulled me close and kissed me until my head spun.

Chapter 17

Ilene's voice cut through my slumber. "Do you know there's a giant egg in your fireplace?"

I tried to sit up, but Valen tightened his hold around my waist. The gesture made me freeze. Oh, right. We were in my bed—together.

"I think they're still sleeping." Although Krissa kept her voice low, my cabin was very small. The words floated to us effortlessly. "You have to try to be quiet."

"But do you think they know the egg is in the fireplace? I wouldn't want them to be caught off guard."

Shuffling sounded downstairs. "I don't think they would miss such a huge egg in their fireplace. I'm sure it's there on purpose."

Silence for a few heartbeats.

"Perhaps they're cooking it, then. Should we cut it open and see if it's done?" Ilene's stomach rumbled, accentuating her point.

"NO!" I jerked upright, Valen's arm falling from me. Bummer, but I couldn't let them casually eat the wyvern egg for breakfast. "Wait! I'll be right down!"

I grabbed a handful of clothes and ducked into the farthest

corner, which remained invisible from below. When I headed toward the ladder, Valen was sitting up in bed. I leaned across the mattress and grabbed his arm.

"What are you doing?" I whispered.

He glanced to one side, then back at me. "Getting up?"

"Absolutely not. I'm not having your sister know you slept in my bed."

A slow grin crawled across his face. My brow creased. He had such pretty lips. It would be a shame if I carved them off his face. At least, that's what I told myself.

He chuckled, but remained quiet. Smart man.

I hurried down the stairs and ran my fingers through my hair at the bottom. Yep, it was a tangled mess. Too late now.

"Good morning." I forced a smile on my face—or at least less of a scowl. "This is not an egg to eat, Ilene, but you're welcome to anything in the kitchen. This is a wyvern egg, I'm fairly sure, and we're trying to see if it was being illegally trafficked."

Ilene, still adorned in her usual armor, stalked into the kitchen with muffled complaints.

But Krissa eyed me.

"I see Valen graduated from the couch," she said flatly.

Heat crawled up my cheeks.

I stammered, "I . . . why . . . what makes you think that?"

She gestured to the couch. It was empty.

I squinted. "So?"

"So? There's been an entire bed made here for the last month. Now look—no bed. Either the mercenary finally packed up and moved out of town, which sounds too good to be true. Or, he's upstairs hiding under your covers."

"He's not hiding," I said. Gods, I could picture Valen's face right now. He loved this, I was sure. "And that's circumstantial.

You have no proof he's in my bed."

She raised a brow. "Your face is brighter than a tomato before canning season. You're really going to make me do it?"

I remained silent. I even crossed my arms as a symbol of fearlessness, although on the inside, I was terrified.

She sighed. "Hey, loser. Are you hiding under Rae's blankets up there or did you finally take the hint and get lost?"

Please don't answer. Please . . .

"I'd hardly classify this as hiding," Valen called back. My heart sank. I pressed both hands over my face and turned away. "I'm merely choosing to remain concealed at the moment."

I didn't need to see Krissa's smug expression. I imagined it in perfect detail.

Ilene's footsteps echoed from the kitchen. She spoke with her mouth full of whatever she'd stolen from my cupboards.

"I wemember my fithrst time." She thankfully swallowed before continuing. "It was a beautiful summer evening. We'd just finished a long battle, and the heat of passion overwhelmed the memories of the battlefield. I'd done my first beheading that fight. Or . . . wait . . . perhaps it was the next night. Either way, every plate of my armor was removed one piece at a time, exposing all of me to—"

"Stop, just stop." I put my hands over my ears. Millions of ways I could die right here, right now, swam through my head. I would have accepted any of them as long as they were quick. "Why are both of you breaking into my house?"

"It's not breaking in now that you've reset the wards. But we have an investigation to complete, unless you've forgotten all about it due to some extracurricular nighttime activities." She wriggled her eyebrows.

Thankfully, Ilene spoke before my silence turned awkward.

"And I must consult with my brother on some rebellion business. I'm afraid there's been another turn in the tides."

The loft creaked as Valen got out of bed. I navigated to the kitchen. Since the day was officially beginning, a strong cup of tea was in order.

Krissa followed me.

"Did you learn anything from the wyvern fire samples?"

"They're not sulfur-based." Valen and I had paused our . . . extracurricular activities . . . long enough for me to conduct some flame tests. "The accelerant used at the crime scene was not wyvern fire."

I pulled out my strongest, most bitter black tea leaves. A dark, smoky scent emitted from the fabric bag, strong enough to wake the dead—which was exactly how I felt. I put the thick glass jar with a whisk attachment beside the tea and set the water boiling in the fireplace.

Krissa's gaze darted to the egg in the flames. "There isn't a mommy wyvern looking for her missing egg, then?"

"Probably not." I hated thinking about what had happened to the little orphan's parents. The poachers either kidnapped the egg or otherwise disposed of its guardians. A painful tug went through my chest. I didn't know what had happened to my parents. Sometimes, when I was alone and my cabin felt quiet, I imagined the people I wanted them to be. That they'd kissed my scraped knees, read me bedtime stories by candlelight. I pretended they fought for me when the king arrived, and only the most dire outcome had prevented them from saving me.

"I think we need to go back to Celeste's butcher shop and ask her about the sulfur." Krissa's voice snapped me out of my thoughts. "I've been thinking about it, and you're probably right. She's almost certainly not involved, but we have to double-check before crossing her off the suspect list. She's honestly the only lead we have right now."

I grimaced. The investigation was crawling due to the wyvern research interruptions.

Rolling bubbles swirled from the pot. I pulled it from the flames and dumped the tea leaves in. The excessive amount was necessary, or Ilene stole all the tea and nobody else got any. I inhaled the thick steam like a lifeline.

"We also need to interrogate the overnight re-stockers at Dollops and Dashes." At least that would feel like progress, even if it didn't lead anywhere. "Toren's autopsy is this afternoon, too."

"I forgot about that! Not the autopsy—ew, gross. Are we doing a stakeout at Dollops and Dashes?"

I took a big spoonful of goat's butter from the bowl and flung it into the glass jar. It spread against the side with a very satisfying splat.

"We're not doing a stakeout. We will be observing the shop until the night workers arrive, and we will politely ask them some questions."

"Oh, baby. I love a good stakeout!"

"It's not . . . oh, never mind." Krissa could call it whatever she wanted, as long as the end result was finally getting some answers about this case.

I set a filter over the mouth of the jar and slowly poured the tea inside. The hot liquid splashed across the white butter, melting it down into a thick layer on the bottom.

"Um, Rae?"

"Yes?"

"You know there's butter in that jar, right?"

"Gasp! You don't say?" I rolled my eyes, set the cauldron

down, and eased the whisk contraption into the jar.

Krissa looked skeptical. "Usually I trust your concoctions explicitly, but this one looks really weird."

I frowned at the beverage. Goat's butter was more white than golden, and softened chunks floated to the top of the tea.

"Good point. I'll add a bit of sugar."

"I don't think that's going to help."

I ignored her, added the sugar, and started vigorously whisking the tea, sugar, butter combination. Within moments, the bitter scent turned lighter as the thick fats and lipids inside the butter eased a foamy texture into the drink. The dark coloration became pale amber, and the mystery chunks disappeared.

Krissa shook her head. "How do you do that?"

I just smiled. "Get us some mugs, please."

Ilene's head jerked our way as soon as I opened the lid. Apparently, important rebellion business could wait for teatime.

I dolled the tea into individual mugs. We each grabbed one and wandered to the living room; Ilene and Krissa took the couch, while Valen and I perched on the mantle with the fire at our backs.

I savored my first sip. The tea was strong but delicate, the complex flavors mellowed by the butter and sugar.

Ahhhh.

"Plans for today, Sunshine?" Valen asked, softly.

I shrugged. "Going to watch Alivia play hide and seek inside some guy's body. Maybe participate in an overnight stakeout later. The usual. What about you?"

"Ha! I told you it was a stakeout!" Krissa high-fived Ilene, who looked a little confused.

The flames danced in his eyes. "I'm going to stay right here and wait for you to come back to me."

Krissa made a gagging noise.

My cheeks heated a little, but a much larger part of me got all warm and tingly.

Chapter 18

The undertaker and I had a rocky start when I first arrived in Hallow's Promise. We'd managed to put our personal differences aside in exchange for a civil, professional relationship. Lately, Alivia had been downright pleasant. She'd performed an illegal autopsy at my request and expedited the blood samples that helped me find Valen when he'd gone missing.

She still unnerved me.

Alivia wore a long, black cloak that covered her from neck to wrists to ankles. It gave the illusion that she floated across the chilled stone floors rather than walked. A thousand mirrors plunged into the underground space, bringing light from the surface into the cold area of the morgue. The silver lights turned her white hair ethereal and made the black mask across her face particularly harsh.

Toren's body looked worse than it had in the forest. His arms and legs pulled tight toward his core, as the muscles had contracted and shortened in the intense heat. Combined with the blackened skin and peeking bone fragments, he barely looked human.

Alivia grabbed the man's leg and jerked it away from the body. It gave with a horrible, sickening crunch.

Castor turned away. He didn't vomit, but his face looked green. Alivia paused her mutilation, I mean . . . examination, to give the marshal's back a disappointed glare.

She finished uncurling the limbs—bones had certainly broken—and exposed the rest of the body.

"I will begin the sternum incision," she said. Her voice was flat, calm, nonchalant. In fact . . . maybe a little gleeful. "Determining the state of the lungs will help reveal the cause of death."

Castor glanced over his shoulder, then quickly away again. Alivia rolled her eyes. The marshal needed to figure out his uneasiness if he wanted the undertaker's respect. Although it was pretty gross.

Alivia's scalpel cut through the flesh with ease, exposing dry, damaged skin before layers of thick, fatty muscles. The putrid scent leaked out once she propped the ribs open. I wrinkled my nose.

The nuances of death were important. Each part was necessary for the continuation of justice and nature. The autopsy exposed the body's hidden secrets. Decomposition allowed the earth's elements to return to the ground. Though they were repulsive and ugly, they were also balance and order.

She reached inside and cradled Toren's right lung. It lifted from the cavity, and her trained scalpel separated it from the rest of his body. The organ was wrinkled, but whole.

Until she sliced it in half.

Oh, my. My stomach rolled. Apparently, splitting organs apart was some sort of line for me.

"Rae, would you care for a closer look?" Alivia's smooth voice echoed through the underground space. No thank you, I do *not* want to look at the severed lung in your hand.

"Sure," I croaked out and stepped closer. What was wrong with me?

She slapped one half of the lung into my hand. It was . . . soft and squishy. Ew, ew, ew . . .

"Do you see these pockets of fluid inside the air sacs?" She gestured with her free hand. "That's indicative of pulmonary edema, common with inhalation of smoke or high heat. And these black specks? Likely soot inhaled during the event."

"Was he killed during the fire or not?" Castor called out. He'd turned back around, but stared hard at his feet.

Alivia was quiet. She was either letting Castor suffer, letting me suffer, or immensely enjoying both at the same time.

"It is my professional opinion that he was killed during the fire. Extreme heat and heat inhalation. There are other signs present, but I will relieve your stress and complete the rest of my examination alone."

She took the lung back. Oh, thank the gods.

Castor mumbled under his breath, probably the same things I was thinking.

Red fluid stained my skin. She hadn't even offered me gloves. I ground my teeth and headed for the basin in the corner. The soap smelled strongly of lye. I scrubbed it into my skin until it felt raw.

Better. Much better.

A crashing sound came from overhead.

Castor and Alivia, who'd been conferring near the bottom of the staircase, paused their conversation and looked upward.

Glass shattered. A thousand shards rained down on us, a deadly cascade of pale raindrops.

We all ducked under cover and away from the exposed center of the room. I may have screamed a bit. It was hard to say.

The glass on the ground shook in place, then darted upright onto their pointed edges. The crystals shot into the air, hesitated halfway up the chamber, then rained down again.

Interesting. Only a few mages could manipulate glass with that precision. Either someone gifted and trained in telekinesis or a geokinetic—able to manipulate earth-based elements.

Either one was just great and almost certainly another special gift from the king.

"I think they're here for me," I said.

"Of course they are," Castor hissed. "Everything that goes wrong in this town is because of you."

I rolled my eyes. Coming from anyone else, that comment would sting. But Castor the Asshole needed much stronger ammunition to strike me.

Heavy footsteps sounded down the stairs as the glass continued to rise and fall. The approached Provider wanted us to remain in place while they made their grand entrance.

No chance of that happening.

"I'll try to incapacitate them as quickly as possible. I'm sorry, Alivia. I'll do my best to protect your morgue."

The undertaker's eyes flashed with a silver glow. She straightened her shoulders and stood from beneath her cover. That starlight gaze locked on me.

"There is no need, necromancer. The time for hiding ended when you defied death. I will stand for Hallow's Promise, which means standing for you."

Alivia stepped into the glass. I screamed, reaching for her, and was rewarded with several blades of glass piercing my skin.

The shards fell around her, but they didn't even scrape her skin. She moved through the crystal assault, her head high, white hair fallen from its bun to cascade around her shoulders.

Alivia looked like a dream—or a nightmare.

The footsteps echoed to the end of the staircase, and the Provider came into view. He was huge. Thick, black armor covered him from head to toe, even keeping his eyes invisible. He studied the room, where the glass continued to slice through the air, but locked onto Alivia alone in the center of the room.

"The necromancer," was all he said. Man of many words.

"I'm afraid she's needed here," Alivia replied, as casual as enjoying a cup of tea.

The Provider lifted his arm. All the shards in the room floated to waist height and pointed directly at Alivia.

"Give her to me."

That silver light expanded in her eyes. A wicked grin spread across her face.

"Take her from me."

I didn't necessarily enjoy being spoken about like an inanimate object, but Alivia's power snapped out in a sharp whip through the room. It was primal, raw, and it stole my breath.

The Provider clenched his fist. All the glass flung toward Alivia, thousands of sharpened pieces aiming directly for her gut.

Her smile widened.

The glass fell. As though hitting an invisible wall inches from her skin, piece after sharpened piece staggered toward the ground in a chorus of snaps and pops.

Alivia was untouched.

"My turn," she said.

That power became cold, colder than Valen's icy touch, consumed by something far more ancient. Instincts cried from my chest that the end was near, and it was complete, beyond anything my powers could resurrect.

Death.

Decay.

Surrender.

Little ghostly shapes flickered at the edge of my vision. They sharpened and solidified, singing a melody of screams and despair. Hands. Dozens of gray, undead hands protruded from the earth. They weren't solid or real. I could feel the touch of my necromancy come alive as Alivia called more and more phantom grips from the earth.

I could take these souls. I felt that. It would hurt, but they could become mine. And something would be lost. These incorporeal bodies had long found peace in the underworld and only responded to very specific types of magic.

Balance was part of death. If I called these souls back into the world, the afterlife would be unbalanced. And that was probably bad.

But the hands had no problems bending to Alivia's will. She did not want to bring them back. No, she was not a crafter of life or death. She simply escorted them.

"A Ferryman," I whispered.

Her gaze swiveled to me. She was gone to the magic.

The hands grabbed the Provider. He screamed, deep and final. They pulled him down and down, the earth easing to make space for his body. Somewhere far in the bowels of the earth, a river waited for him. Eventually, a Ferryman would arrive and escort him across, into the great unknown.

His armor clanked to the ground.

It was empty.

Alivia's eyes faded. She swayed and fell.

Castor ran to the undertaker, and I followed close behind. He cradled her in his arms, and Alivia's gray eyes flickered open.

I sat back. Relief flooded through me. She was fine, just exhausted after the expenditure of power.

"Ferrymen are illegal," I said.

She chuckled, weak and thin. "So are necromancers."

I studied her. Our original conflict made sense now. Our magics were basically siblings, and like all siblings, they bickered. Combine that with a dash of fearing for our lives and a hint of death, it was lucky we hadn't destroyed anything until today.

"Thank you." I poured everything unspoken into the word. Thank you for not reporting me to Erline when my very existence here threatened your life. Thank you for understanding me in a way that nobody else ever will. Thank you for exposing your secret too, so I'm not alone.

"Anytime, Rae. Though . . . perhaps not for a few more hours."

Chapter 19

"*Alivia* has death magic, too?" Krissa pouted. "That's totally not fair. Leof is a werewolf. Valen is basically half necromancer. The undertaker is a Ferryman into the afterlife. And me? I'm good with numbers! *That's not a power!*"

"What about the power of friendship?" I asked.

Oops. That was not the right thing to say.

"That's a nice way of saying '*no powers.*'" She quickly wiped her eyes. Oh, no, was she crying? I didn't do well with crying people. They made me uncomfortable and a little afraid.

"Look, Alivia is a Ferryman, Leof's a werewolf, Valen is . . . well Valen, and Suzie can launch fireballs from her hands."

"Oh, yes, thank you, I forgot about the *teenager.*"

Suzie was young, but not a teenager. I bit my lip instead of correcting her. Krissa was clearly going through something at the moment.

"But none of them are here! Look around. You're the only one I asked to participate in the stakeout tonight. Why do you think that is?"

She pouted, which looked very endearing on her round face. "Because I'm the only one crazy enough to come with you?"

That wasn't completely wrong. "It's because you look at the

world differently than anyone else. You see people for who they are and not how they want to be seen. If I need someone dead, I'll bring Valen. When I need insight on what people are trying to hide from me, you're the first person I'm going to ask."

She crossed her arms. "That's not even true."

"I know it is."

"How?"

I blinked. Did she really not know? Krissa turned her beautiful brown eyes—brimming with silver teardrops—toward me and studied my face. One droplet flooded over the rim and painted a single shining line down her cheek.

I'd never had friends as a child. The king's soldiers surrounded me constantly. I shared a room with a nursemaid, who also had a dagger tattooed on her forearm. Being truly alone for the first time had terrified me—until I realized it brought freedom. Freedom from judgement, demands, pain, everything.

Until it didn't.

Once I settled in Hallow's Promise, I wanted to be alone. Leof had been my first friend. He'd pulled me out of my shell, given me a house and a job.

But Krissa was the first person I had chosen to be my friend.

"Because you saw me." I grabbed both of her arms. "When I wanted the world to turn away, you saw me. And you're still here."

Her objects faded. The tears in her eyes remained, but her lips tugged upward into a smile. Without warning, she flung both of her arms tight around me. Her lye soap scent fluttered around me, familiar and comforting. I'd tried to mix her specific scent into a tea once—a little citrus and some orange blossom—but it never came out quite right. Maybe it was missing the warm hug part.

"Thank you, Rae. I needed to hear that." She pulled back and smiled.

"Anytime, Krissa. And I mean it. Now, where should we start this stakeout?"

Her eyes grew wide. "You're asking me?"

"I'm taking a break from making plans."

"That's what I'm talking about." She rubbed her hands together and I sort of instantly regretted giving her a taste of control. "I think we should lay down in those bushes in the back. That gives us a clear view of both the front and rear doors without being completely obvious."

I eyed the bushes. "Okay, but why are we hiding? It's not illegal to wait for overnight employees to start their shift."

"If one of them is the perp, they're going to run as soon as they see you."

"I don't think anyone will recognize me."

"Are you serious? Everyone knows you now. If they don't recognize you, they'll certainly recognize *him*." She gestured to Bubbles. He glanced at her extended palm, then back to me with his beady little eyes. He flicked his long tongue out to lick one eyeball—just one. "Nobody else has a pet warplog. Why did you bring him, anyway?"

I shrugged. "He's nocturnal, so he was awake. And he looked lonely."

"I don't think he's nocturnal. What's it called when something sleeps all the time?"

"Alright, we'll do it your way. We'll go hide in the bushes."

Krissa bounced on her toes and clapped. "I can't wait. An actual, real-life stakeout. Do you know how rare this is?"

"I mean, I've never done one."

"Eeek!" She grabbed my hands. "We get to share our first time *together*. I am so excited!"

***

"I am so bored." Krissa snapped another branch from the bush we'd crawled under hours ago. At this point, they were mostly sticks hanging onto a slightly thicker stock. She pulled all the leaves off and crumpled them into dust, one by one. "This is your fault. You didn't tell me that a stakeout would be so boring."

"I never said it was a stakeout." But it had been a long night. Bubbles had slept almost the entire time. He'd groaned and complained a bit when I refused to let him sleep on me. I shifted positions on the hard ground continuously. Adding a warplog would make comfort impossible. But he'd moved some dirt around with his oversized hind legs and curled into a little warplog ball beside me. It was actually super cute, though he would require a bath when we got home.

"You also didn't say that we'd be sleeping on the ground." Krissa had gotten pieces of sleep throughout the night, though admittedly not much.

"We could have gone to the Sorrow and rented a corner room to watch the shop."

The Siren's Sorrow was an old inn on Main Street. Its clientele consisted mostly of criminals, but since that description included me due to the capital's official decree, I couldn't throw stones. Besides, it was better than marinating in the mud all night and showering in debris of crumpled leaves.

Krissa's head swiveled like a possessed owl. "That was an option?"

I shrugged. "Why not?"

"That's it. I'm done." Krissa scooted on her elbows until finally clearing the bushes and crouching onto her knees. She peered back at me, still lounging in my muddy spot.

"Planning is harder than it looks, huh?"

Her eyes narrowed. "Was this all to teach me a lesson? You let us lay in the bushes all night to prove that your plans don't suck? Well, I have news for you. Just because my plans also suck, doesn't mean yours are any better!"

"I agree." Shimming out of the shrubs proved harder than expected. My joints complained, and I suddenly had to use the bathroom *very* badly. I carefully pulled Bubbles from his dirt nest, wrapped him in the shawl I'd previously sacrificed to serve as a pillow, and cradled him in my arms. He didn't move. "I don't think the night workers are showing up. Let's go."

Krissa grabbed my arm. "Wait!"

I followed her gaze.

A shadow moved along the stone exterior of Dollops and Dashes. It was short, but quick, and confident. The shadow turned into a figure, who paused at the rear door, and fiddled with the lock.

"I think someone's breaking in," Krissa whispered.

I glanced around. Technically, night had ended hours ago. It was that awkward time where the sun hadn't risen yet, but the promise of dawn hovered on the horizon. The perfect time for recreational mischief.

The lock snapped open.

"You have to go stop them."

I glanced behind me. Surely, there must have been some law enforcement officer hovering around that I simply hadn't noticed.

No, Krissa was looking at me.

"I'm not a constable. I don't apprehend people."

"If you don't do something, the intruder is going to get away. This could be the murderer! Maybe throw Bubbles in there. He'll probably do something."

Yeah, something like snoring loudly or spilling acid drool all over Brynn's floor.

"I thought you were convinced that Celeste is the killer?"

"It could be her! We won't know if you don't go in there and find out."

"Why don't you do it?"

She gestured to herself, then to me. "Hello, no powers, remember? If I had a magic sword and death magic, you bet I'd be in there already!"

The world was not ready for a magical Krissa.

"Okay, I'll go look. Here, hold this." I passed Bubbles over. The warplog lazily cracked one eye open, grumbled about his disrupted nap, and went back to sleep. I envied him.

I pulled my sword. It had decided not to smoke at the moment, which was fine. Really, it was. I didn't need any magical help anyway, and I was not at all angry about it.

The sounds of drawers opening and closing escaped through the ajar door as I stepped closer. Fresh scents oozed outside. A little earthy, slightly bitter, but generally unconcerning. If I got a whiff of sulfur, I planned to grab Krissa and run. After watching Toren's autopsy, I decided to avoid burning to death if at all possible.

I pressed my back against the stone wall and nudged the door open more. A soft glow illuminated the shop. The intruder had . . . lit a candle?

Steps came closer to the door. I tensed. I had one opportunity to nab this suspect before they became aware of my presence. Time slowed. All my senses opened as I tracked the movement, the anticipation, my breath, and everything in between.

The figure covered the candlelight.

I launched through the door. It slammed into the exterior wall with a crash and a bang. Several smaller jars fell from the shelves, but thankfully none of them broke. Dealing with shattered glass during a fight was literally the worst.

The figure beneath me gasped. They wore a brown hooded cloak, and thrust their arms inside it, looking sort of lost in the fabric.

I pulled the hood back and pressed my sword against the stranger's neck.

Large, clear eyes looked back at me. Her lips formed round circles, and I already saw a line of tears building across her lashes.

I drew the sword back and sheathed it.

"I am so sorry," I stammered, holding out a hand.

Krissa's head peeked inside. "Did you get them? Is it Celeste? I knew it. I knew I didn't trust her."

"No, Krissa, it's not Celeste. It's Brynn, and I just attacked her in her own shop."

Chapter 20

"I am so sorry," I repeated for the hundredth time.

Brynn waved my words away. She'd wrapped the cloak around her shoulders and cradled a cup of tea I'd quickly prepared with supplies from her shop. I paid for all of them, of course. It wasn't her fault for being slammed into the ground and held at swordpoint over a misunderstanding.

"Don't worry, Rae. I'm glad to have people watching my back. If there was an intruder in my shop, that's exactly what I hope will happen to them."

"Well, I'm still sorry."

She took another sip. Brynn was shorter than me and wore an assortment of hooped jewelry that released soft jingles when she moved her head.

"What were you doing here at this hour, anyway?"

"We're working on a case and trying to narrow down business and individuals purchasing sulfur locally. Your shop was on the list, so we talked to your cousin a couple of days ago."

Her eyes widened, then narrowed. "You spoke to Eleric? He didn't mention that."

"He said you were at River's Edge setting up a new shop.

When I asked about your sulfur stock, he told me to check with the night employees because they're the ones that restock the shelves."

Brynn snorted. "What night employees? I'm the only one who restocks the shelves, Rae. Oh, I am going to kill that boy when I find him."

I tensed, and Krissa stilled beside me. "You don't have any night staff?"

"No, it's just me."

"Sito or Veric?"

"I've never heard those names in my life. I asked Eleric to manage the shop because I don't have any other options. The only person coming into this place when the sun is down is me."

Krissa jumped up. "Eleric killed Toren! And he lied to cover up his involvement. I knew it! I should have trusted my instincts."

"You thought Veric committed the murder. Also, let's remember we're talking about Brynn's family members. Let's not accuse them of a crime without any evidence."

"Oh, right." My friend grimaced. "Sorry, Brynn."

"Do you . . . you think he *killed* someone?" She pressed her hands to her mouth. "How? Can you tell me how?"

I shook my head and put my hand on her arm. "I'm sorry, but that's confidential to the investigation. I do have some questions, if you feel able to answer them?"

She nodded.

"Do you know who he could be working with?" I asked. "We think this might be part of a larger illegal animal trading ring."

"Look, Eleric has a troubled history, and it's not completely surprising that he'd get caught with the wrong group. But he's not exactly a 'go-getter,' if you know what I mean. While he's good at following orders, he's not going to plan an elaborate crime circuit by himself."

"Where should we look for him, Brynn?"

Her throat bobbed. "If he hasn't skipped town, he'll be at his mom's house. They live in Devote Alcove, near the park."

I squeezed her arm. "Thank you. I'm so sorry to intrude in your life like this. I hope we can resolve everything peacefully, and maybe it's all a misunderstanding."

"Thanks, Rae. I'll . . . see you around."

We left Brynn in her shop and softly closed the door.

"I was not expecting that," Krissa whispered. "We probably talked to the killer first. That never happens!"

"Don't get excited yet. We don't know how Eleric is involved in this, or even really know where he is. I have to stop at the station and get his mom's address from Leof." Bubbles snored in Krissa's arms. "He can sleep in my new office while we look for Eleric."

She tilted her head. "New office?"

"Come on, I'll show you." I winked and headed toward the sheriff's station.

* * *

The front desk was empty. Last time I'd been annoyed about the interrogation required to enter the building. Today, it was sad. The constable charged with protecting the front doors had died because of me.

If I'd been keeping a list, it would have been long.

The rest of the station had recovered. The ash and charred bits were cleared, and the walls repainted, only a smoky metallic smell remained. Constables milled around the halls.

My heart clenched. None of these people were safe. War was upon us.

Someone ran into my back. I staggered with a grunt, and the offender gave half a laugh.

Castor. I recognized the bile in his voice anywhere.

I turned, a biting remark on my tongue.

It faded as I realized he dragged another person behind him.

"Looks like I had to step in and do your job, witch." He pulled the woman forward.

Celeste bared her teeth at him. He had her hands shackled behind her back, but she straightened her spine and jerked her chin up. Her eyes met mine, and a bit of the light faded from her irises. She thought I was involved in this.

Rage bubbled inside me.

"What did you do, Castor?" I whispered.

"I did what you're incapable of. I investigated a crime, found a suspect, and will be presenting her for trial in a fortnight. You can enjoy that big office, the sheriff's favor, but remember that you're nothing behind all of that. You're an illegal outcast that only brings trouble to this town."

I let his words roll off me. Later, I could focus on them, analyze every part and decide which ones I believed. But not right now.

"Well, you're an asshole," Krissa said.

Holy . . . A laugh burst from my lips—more of a harsh grunt.

Castor eyed us, his lips pressed into a scowl. He rolled his eyes and pulled Celeste down the hall. She didn't complain.

"Stop, stop!" I followed him, but he didn't slow his pace.

"What evidence do you have for this arrest?"

"Her store is registered as a purchaser of sulfur, but when I went in for an inspection, the inventory was drained. Apparently, they don't keep logs of their stock, and she didn't realize they'd run out. Or . . ." He stopped in front of his office door. The jail cells below the station had been accidentally demolished during a previous case, forcing most prisoners to be retained in personal offices until they were transported to Erline to serve their sentence. Hm . . . I wondered where they went now that Hallow's Promise and the capital were separated. "She used the rest in an accelerant to burn someone alive."

I crossed my arms. "Why would Celeste do that? What's the motive?"

He shrugged. "Illegal animal trade might be bad for the meat business. I don't know, but I have enough evidence to detain her while I search the house and shop."

"That's lovely, Castor. Really, you're showing all the qualities of a great person. Tell me, are you going to restrain her elderly father, too?"

An evil spark danced in his eye. "You know what, witch, that's a great idea. As soon as I'm done with her interrogation, the old man is next. Adding a little pressure might even make a confession come faster, huh, sweetheart?" He glanced at Celeste. "Would you tell me the truth if it meant securing your father's freedom? Enough talking. Come on."

He pulled her into the doorway and tried to slam it closed. I stuck my foot inside, and the door whacked my toes but didn't close. Ouch, it did hurt a little.

"I'm going to fix this," I told the butcher.

Celeste didn't smile, but her gaze softened.

Castor pulled her in and stood at the crack in the door.

"You can't fix anything. This town is broken because *you* are broken. If you want things to be better, then—"

I pulled my foot out of the door, and it slammed shut in his face. That was satisfying.

Krissa, Bubbles, and I went into my office. She set the warplog onto one of the chairs. He rolled over and went back to sleep.

"I know I liked Celeste as a suspect, but now that Castor has the same thought, I totally hate it."

"We've never had any proof that Celeste was involved. We know that Eleric lied about the night employees at the store. He's a much stronger suspect."

"Agreed. What now?"

"I'm going to ask Leof where Eleric's mother lives. We both need some sleep, then we'll go see if he's home."

"And you'll bring Valen this time?"

I smiled. "Of course."

Leof's head drooped over his desk when I stepped into his office. It smelled like him—woodsy, leather, wolf. But it didn't look like him yet. The room was too cold and sterile. Too much rough wood and red paint.

He lifted his head when the door clicked into the lock.

"I didn't mean to wake you," I said.

He stood, slow, like he ached. "It's fine. I haven't slept yet and must have dozed off."

"We have that in common."

"You didn't sleep either?" He arched his brow.

"Nope." And now that he mentioned it, a sickly feeling churned my stomach and my eyelids grew heavy. I needed to sleep—soon.

"Do I want to know why not?"

I shrugged. "It was investigative work. You management people wouldn't understand." That got me a snort, at least. "Castor arrested an innocent person in the murder case we're working on."

"Sorry, that sounds like an investigative issue. I wouldn't understand."

"Ha, ha. You might want to understand if this goes to trial, and he has to admit to the entire town that he's an asshole. Actually, that doesn't sound like such a bad idea."

"If Castor arrested the wrong person, I'm sure you're on your way to correct him right now. Do you need something from me, or are you just here to complain? Either one is fine, but I can probably only stay awake for one of them."

I eyed the werewolf. He had circles under his eyes, and his hair was unwashed. Actually, the wolf smell was slightly stronger than the rest of his usual scents. Running the town and attempting to avoid Providers breaching the walls must have been challenging him.

"I need someone's address," I said softly.

"Finally, something I can actually help with. Give me the name and I'll find the house."

I did. He plopped back into his chair and fished out a giant book. The Hallow's Promise town ledger. It listed every resident's address, with fairly high accuracy. I told him the names, and he ran his finger down the list. A pen and parchment appeared, and he jotted the location down.

"Thanks, Leof. Get some sleep."

"You, too."

He winked at me, and I smiled back.

Things had changed. Hallow's Promise would never be the same. When the war came, we'd either band together or tear each other apart. Decisions and consequences loomed in the distance and drew closer every day.

But right now, I had the next location for my investigation, an innocent woman to free from imprisonment, and good friends at my back.

And also, I needed a nap.

Chapter 21

"Do you want to come with us to interrogate our new suspect?" I asked.

A sword swung through the air. Loose strands of my hair brushed across my face as I barely moved back to avoid the strike. While the dull training blade probably wouldn't kill me, it would give me a killer headache. I, unfortunately, knew that from experience.

I used my momentum to swing a backward strike toward Valen. The mercenary stepped away effortlessly, leaving a trail of dark smoke in his wake.

Show off.

"Are you asking for my help with an investigation?"

He dropped onto one knee and swept my feet out from under me with the other leg. I sucked in a breath, let it out as my side impacted the ground, and rolled away before his blade landed where my head had been.

The adrenaline dumped into my veins, and my mind cleared. It was so easy to focus while sparring. The troubles and fears of the world couldn't penetrate the circle of stones that designated our fighting area.

Valen and I had a lot of history within this dirt circle. I'd trapped him inside under threat of death, and he'd promised to tell me all his secrets. Then, he'd disappeared. He'd died. And I brought him back to life.

"I think *help* is an exaggeration." I found my footing. Sweat spilled down my back and soaked my light cotton tunic. I lifted my sword, and Valen mirrored me. "I really just need a big, strong man to intimidate this suspect, but I couldn't find one, so I'm asking you."

He put one hand over his heart. The way he held the sword loosely with the other made my heart speed up and my throat go dry.

"You wound me, Sunshine."

We circled each other.

The afternoon sun looked good on Valen. It illuminated the hidden shades among his dark, stranded locks. The golden reflection warmed his crystal eyes. It made that half-smile even more mouthwatering.

He *moved* too fast. I reacted a moment too late. The cold tip of his sword brushed the base of my throat.

Each pulse of my heart bounced against the metal. His gaze shifted to the place where the sword touched my skin. That part of me warmed and spread through my body. Frantic butterflies tried to escape my stomach, but my throat was far too tight.

"You did that on purpose," I whispered.

He tilted his head. "What? Distract you with my dashingly good looks? I'm afraid that was of your own doing, Sunshine."

"You used magic to move faster."

"Your words are sharp today. Maybe I used magic, or maybe I'm just that good." He winked.

I rolled my eyes. "I know you used magic—I felt it."

During my escape from Erline, I'd killed several people and pushed all their life magic into Valen as my personal puppet. They taught me that nobody could sustain that amount of power—it would rip them apart from the inside out.

Well, it turns out that people in power like to craft lies in order to keep that power. The king and his Providers had lied to me. That man hadn't died. He'd cut down every enemy between me and my freedom. At the final moment, I abandoned him and left him for dead.

That man had been Valen.

During the exchange, some of my magic had transferred into him. He'd spent his years of freedom manipulating and honing his new skills, while I learned to make potions and hid from the capital. While he couldn't defy life and death, he could Smoke-Wield and harness the micro-life between two spaces to move faster or travel long distances. Plenty of life existed between him and a target, which he used to move quickly.

And right now, I was his target.

A twinkle lit in his eyes. My cheeks instantly burned. I recognized that look.

"Don't you . . ."

He dipped the knife lower. Although the edges were dull, it was sharp enough to cut through the front of my thin tunic in a moment. I gasped as spring air touched my skin.

Valen smirked and reversed the strike.

My top fell apart into two large chunks. I squealed—yes, legitimately squealed—and grabbed at the edges of the fabric before exposing my undergarments to the world.

Valen's hand stopped mine. He drew me close, the feel of his warmth erasing all my concerns. His bare chest erased the cool air. The places where we touched sent sparks up and down my spine.

He put his lips against my ear. "Tell me what I want to hear, Sunshine."

No air. No words.

"You win," I said. My mind was blank. I didn't remember how to speak, but at least those words sounded coherent.

He chuckled. "No. Tell me you need my help, Sunshine."

Oh, that cut straight through the fog of desire. I pulled back. "Never."

"Can you be serious for one moment?"

"Also, never."

"Listen, Sunshine." He pulled me in again and tucked my head under his chin. Our magic touched—ice and flames. "I need to hear you say it because I don't want to intrude on your life. I want to be a partner, a helper, and part of that is responding to what you ask from me. Your investigations are your own—unless you want them to be ours."

"Valen, I am so sick of this heart-to-heart stuff. You are not overstepping. I want your help, and I'm going to need it all the time. Please stop talking and . . . just kiss me already."

"No more heart-to-heart? Alright then." He pushed my head back and kissed my neck. "There are two other things I'd rather put together, anyway."

I couldn't breathe around this man. There was something else we were supposed to be doing . . . something important . .

.

"Murder!" I squeaked.

Valen raised his head from my neck. "Is that a threat?"

"Probably not. But we have to investigate a murder. Then, we can get back to . . . this."

His grip loosened. My body complained, and, well, so did

my mind. But once this investigation was over, I'd have Valen all to myself. And also the war efforts—which I was trying to ignore.

He ran his finger along my lower lip and hesitated at the corner. Sharp tingles spread across my face.

"I'll make sure you keep that promise."

* * *

Changing my clothes had required a further delay, but I couldn't interrogate Eleric in my bralette.

Ilene and Kriss joined us, which created a weird little posse. Ilene wore her usual worn armor, freshly adorned with a new splash of blood after her recent visit to the front lines. Krissa wore an ankle-length rainbow skirt, and the wisp of a red ribbon in her hair looked suspiciously similar to Ilene's stain. They held hands in the evening sunlight. A warrior and a professor, two worlds mashed into one.

"What was that?" Valen asked from beside me.

"What?"

"That sigh. What was it for?"

"I didn't sigh."

"Yes, you did, with a disgusting whimsical longing that I'm fairly certain had nothing to do with me. Which is quite a shame. I expect to be the reason for all your whimsical longing from now on."

I tried to shove him, but he caught my hand. Our arms slowly lowered, fingers still connected. I waited for him to pull away.

Surely a hardened mercenary like Valen didn't *hold hands*. But he didn't let go.

Since Valen had returned to life, I thought I'd identified all the places in my heart that had been broken and repaired so many times. There was a permanent hole where my parents should be. A piece of me that Krissa's friendship filled perfectly. Bubbles had a tiny nest right near the center. Surely, I couldn't have much space left in such a malnourished heart.

Again—I was wrong.

This touch was tender, kind, lingering. It wasn't eager and demanding—which I admittedly had been enjoying—but intimate, confident. If someone he knew from his other roles appeared on this road, I knew Valen's hand wouldn't let go of mine—unless he needed to grab a sword, perhaps.

And that made the rest of my heart melt.

I glanced at the man holding my hand. He didn't look at me, but he was smiling.

The road turned, spilling us onto the intersection of Reverence Square and Devote Alcove. Hallow's Promise was layered. The north side of town housed the residents with fewer options in life—less money and more substance abuse problems. Main Street cut across the center, with the wealthiest families housed in palaces on the south side of town. Devote Alcove was somewhere in the middle. People made do with what they had, but they had a lot more than some others.

Except . . . we turned left, into Reverence Square.

"I think we're going the wrong way," I said.

Valen paused. He glanced at the slip of parchment bearing the address Leof had provided.

"No, this is the right way."

I creased my brow. Valen had a house hidden in the debris of

Reverence Square. He used poverty as a cover for his hidden lair. Valen knew the area better than I did. He wouldn't turn us the wrong way. But . . .

"Brynn said her cousin lives in Devote Alcove."

"The address from Leof goes this way. Maybe Brynn was confused, or maybe our target moved, and no one updated the ledger. Either way, we have to search this place first."

"Okay." I let Valen pull me forward. Makeshift structures hobbled into rough houses. Parts of some walls crumbled down, revealing a layer of filth from inside. It smelled yeasty and sad. People eyed us on the streets, but nobody spoke a word. I knew Valen tried to help those willing to accept it—but most of these people didn't want out of their ruins. They used it as a shield from the real world.

We finally reached the corner of the road, where it ended along the edge of a tree line. One short house stood on the left side. The walls were intact, the roof didn't have any holes, and a row of fresh laundry floated in the breeze.

A familiar tingle ran up my spine.

My magic crawled out from my chest. It slipped around the house, savoring the flavor.

Valen's gaze snapped to me. "What's wrong?"

The coils of magic sang to me. I hadn't been exercising my power very much, but I already knew that a dead person felt very different from everything else. The potential, the loss, the pure power was thicker and more tempting to consume.

I drew my magic away.

"Death," I said. "Someone is dead in this house."

Chapter 22

We all stared at the front door. Each of us had a relationship with death in our own way. None of us wanted to open the door.

"Is it Brynn?" Krissa asked. "Can you at least tell me if it's Brynn?"

I shook my head. "I'm sorry, but I can't tell."

"Are you sure it's a person? Maybe they lost a pet this morning, or a mouse accidentally crawled into the fireplace. I mean, I wouldn't want to see a dead mouse either, but that would be preferable to the alternatives."

My stomach twisted. If Brynn decided to confront Eleric before we arrived, it very much could be her body in that house.

Valen touched my hand. "Do you want me to go look?"

"No." I straightened my shoulders. "I'll go check. It should be me."

My feet didn't want to budge from the rough road, but I forced them forward. Each step drew me closer to the pulsing power of death inside the house. It felt fresh and new, maybe hours since life had departed.

The front stoop used to have a cover, which had long ago slumped to the side and fallen in a cascade of wood and debris.

Boards secured the windows—a necessity in this part of town. The stench of decay hadn't started seeping from the cracks yet. Funny, how the littlest things made me feel grateful sometimes.

I knocked. It felt silly to rap my knuckles against the splintering wood door when I knew nothing alive lingered in the house, but I did it anyway. My taps echoed and met only silence.

Now or never.

I twisted the knob, and it opened without protest. The entryway was small, leading to a smaller living area with a tiny kitchen tucked into the rear of the house. A wood stove doubled as a stovetop and a heater for the winter nights. Two doors split off the living room, probably a bedroom and washroom. The blanket draped across the couch suggested that it doubled as a bed.

And that's where the body was.

Krissa stood on her tiptoes and stared over my shoulder.

"Well, that's not Brynn."

His eyes were open but glazed. Whatever they looked at stretched far beyond our world. Blood stained his tunic along the edges of linear cuts across the fabric. Without touching the body, it appeared as though someone had stabbed him, and he woke up before the death blow. His lips were pale, blue, and frozen into a permanent gasp.

And it certainly wasn't Brynn.

"Let me guess." Valen stepped inside the house. His gaze bounced back and forth, always waiting for the next threat. "This is the cousin."

Eleric was dead.

"Yes," I said. "There goes my best suspect in this case."

"Only suspect," Krissa pointed out.

"Great, thanks."

Illene walked through the rest of the house. She returned to the living room and shrugged. "Any man that does not prepare for an ambush in his sleep deserves to be stabbed to death."

Krissa patted her hand. "That's a little harsh, love."

"It doesn't make any sense." I circled the room. A bit of blood flicked across the wall behind the couch—a pattern that matched the stab wounds well enough. No marks marred the stained rugs across the ground. This was a clean kill. "Eleric clearly wasn't the one in charge of this illicit animal trading operation. If the leader had wanted to kill him after ordering him to burn Toren, they would have done it right away. Why wait all this time?"

"Maybe they assumed he'd get away with it," Krissa said. "We didn't even suspect him until this morning."

"Nobody else knows we suspected him. The sheriff's station has formally accused Celeste of the crime. There's no reason to kill Eleric now." I swirled all the information around in my head, but none of the pieces snapped into place.

"Celeste's shop was out of sulfur. That's suspicious." Krissa stuck one finger out, quickly followed by another. "She hates the animal trade—which could be the motive. But she also wants out of the butcher business, and being in jail would really minimize her other options."

I looked back at the dead guy. His lifeless mouth tried to scream, to yell, but it wasn't really fear frozen on his face. There weren't any defensive wounds on his hands. Either he hadn't had time to raise them or . . .

Of course.

The windows were boarded up, but the door had been unlocked. Nobody in Reverence Square would leave their doors unlocked, especially while they were asleep. The perpetrator must have had a key to get into the house and didn't bother locking up on their way out. They knew there was nobody inside to protect anymore.

If Eleric recognized the person attacking him, it may have distracted him long enough for the fatal injuries to occur, leaving him little to no time to defend himself. He would be confused and surprised, but not necessarily afraid.

"He knew his attacker," I said.

We all thought about that for a minute.

Krissa shook her head. "That still doesn't make sense. We're the only ones who suspected Eleric. Nobody else knew."

"But that's not right, is it? One other person knew we were planning on talking to Eleric. She gave us the wrong location to try to throw us off the trail."

Krissa straightened. "Her shop was completely out of sulfur—not because a client bought it all but—"

"Because she used it to burn Toren!"

Krissa grabbed my hands and jumped up and down. "You did it! You figured it out!"

"Care to share with the group?" Valen asked.

"It's Brynn!" I shouted. "I don't know why yet, but she killed Toren, burned the scene to cover it up, then killed her cousin when we started getting too close to the truth."

"Good job, Sunshine. Now you've just got to figure out how to catch her."

"Hopefully she's not long gone by now." Krissa tapped her finger against her chin. "Eleric said Brynn has a new shop in River's Edge."

Hm, if she were smart, she'd have fled the city right after offing Eleric. We couldn't leave the town without being immediately arrested and brought to Erline for treason—which would defeat everything we'd been trying to do.

"We need to lead her back into Hallow's Promise," I said. What did an animal trader want badly enough to risk returning to the scene of a crime?

A slow smile crawled across my lips. Valen raised his brows.

"Something like a wyvern egg?"

"Exactly. And a really fat warplog."

Chapter 23

Dymetri looked better than last time I saw him. His dark hair had grown out and mostly covered his ears. His face had refilled, although a hollowness lingered in his eyes. He smiled when we approached his place among the shadows.

The lights of the Siren's Sorrow illuminated him from behind. A soft sound of conversation followed by an occasional yell gave our meeting the perfect air of cover. Oil lanterns flickered along the sides of the roads. All the elements were in place for a lovely springtime evening.

"I spread the rumors of an extremely rare, enhanced male warplog down the proper channels. I did mention the wyvern egg too, but I'll be honest, it didn't get nearly as much attention. Apparently, that thing is in high demand."

Dy pointed at Bubbles, who lounged in my arms.

I looked down. Enhanced? That was a generous description for the extra rolls spilling off my arms as he happily snored in his sleep.

"I guess fat warplogs are hard to come by. One person said they have to eat about three adult bodies per week to overwhelm the speed of their natural metabolism. I imagine it's hard for most people to have so many dead people readily available."

I glanced at Valen from the corner of my eye. He didn't look at me. Coward.

"Is the rest of the plan in place?"

"Yep. Here's the location." Dy passed on a square of parchment. "Meeting's at midnight. Whoever shows will get to participate in the auction. I warn you—this isn't a group you want to piss off. If they're bidding on a fat warplog and don't get one, they're going to be up in arms."

Valen's eyes sparkled. "Good," he said.

"Alright, give him here." Dy held out his arms. I squeezed Bubbles a little closer to me. I'd asked him very nicely if he minded being the bait for our trap tonight, and he'd licked both of his eyes and burped, which probably meant he was fine with it. I wasn't really worried about him. If Bubbles decided he didn't like his accommodations, he'd just eat the person causing him problems. But even the possibility of putting him in danger made my heart ache.

I held the warplog up—barely. He really was heavy. His little eyes opened lazily, mostly annoyed that I'd disturbed his slumber.

"You be careful," I told him.

Nothing. Not even a squint. Fine.

I put him in Dymetri's arms. The man groaned and widened his stance.

"He is a bit thick, isn't he?"

I ignored him. "Make sure he stays safe. If anything happens to that warplog, your head will adorn my fireplace, and your body will feed the baby wyvern when it hatches."

Dy smiled. The look faded when he saw my face and replaced it with a solemn nod.

"He'll be safe, I promise. Be in the crowd at midnight and blend in. I'll see you there."

Dy's cloak swirled as he tucked Bubbles under one arm and spun around into the darkness.

Valen rubbed my arm. I bit my lip.

"Bubbles will be okay," Valen whispered into my ear. His voice soothed some of my worries, though not all. "And if there's even a scratch on the creature, I'll teach you how to skin Dymetri. He'd make a lovely leather coat."

I laughed and grimaced simultaneously, but his words had their effect. Together, Valen and I would make sure Bubbles came home tonight, safe and sound.

* * *

"I've never been to an evil auction before," I told Valen as we walked toward the location Dy had provided. I'd donned a long black cape and set the hood over my head. I didn't like wearing hoods. The king demanded his Providers wear cloaks, and I found that a lifetime in the darkness no longer appealed to me. But if Brynn showed up at this auction, we needed the element of surprise to capture her.

"Really? I thought that would be your guilty pleasure, Sunshine."

I elbowed him in the ribs, but didn't have the energy to do much more. The worry I felt for Bubbles gnawed at my gut.

"Does Bubbles think I abandoned him?" I bit my lip.

"I don't think he even woke up from his nap," Valen said.

Dymetri hosted his illegal auction at the edge of The Void.

I shivered as I remembered the House Spider and wyvern fighting and all those strings of power and life that connect this stretch of forest to those that dwelt inside. Hopefully, they'd all stay put tonight, or at least eat the evil animal poachers and not me or Valen.

A small crowd hid among the shadows. Dy hadn't exaggerated—Bubbles was in high demand.

Valen arched a brow at me. The crowd apparently surprised him, too. He squeezed my hand once and disappeared into the throng. We'd discussed all our options and decided that splitting up gave us the best opportunity of finding Brynn. Of course, that assumed she was actually here.

I knew she'd show up. Even if she suspected this to be some kind of trap, her temptation for animals had grown beyond common sense. She and Toren had stolen a wyvern egg. Someone didn't do that unless they were too deep in the game to claw their way back out.

"Good evening, my fine ladies. Ah, and there are some gentlemen here, too. Welcome, welcome." Dymetri started the presentation. His voice boomed loudly enough to be heard, but low enough to avoid inviting unwanted guests, such as the city guards. If any of the constables discovered our gathering, the information would go straight to Castor. I needed to have solid evidence clearing Celeste's name before the marshal showed up and screwed everything.

Dy started again. "Tonight I offer a rare prize, only recently acquired and in my possession for less than one sunrise." He thrust Bubbles from under his cloak and up into the air. The warplog's eyes bulged as he judged his proximity to the ground. A little hiccup escaped his throat. The crowd all sighed. He was pretty cute. "This is a rare male warplog, well fed as you can see. I'm assured he completes his expected twenty hours of daily slumber and eats only the finest decayed flesh. He is in excellent condition."

Bubbles halfheartedly wiggled one of his back legs in protest and gave up when he couldn't even reach around his expanded belly to kick Dy's hands. That settled it. As soon as this nonsense was over, Bubbles was going on a diet. One rotten cow leg per week—no more.

The recap of Bubbles' excellent condition continued, but I turned my attention to the crowd. Most people also wore hoods pulled over their faces. Faded light from distant lanterns splashed across enough features to determine that none of those near me were Brynn.

I shifted my hood. The thick wool brushed my cheek, and old memories resurfaced. I'd worn a cloak every day in Erline. The king's voice echoed in my ears. My hands started shaking as a part of my chest tried to close up. I gasped for air—I needed to breathe, but my lungs refused.

Smoke coils wrapped around my hands. I'd clamped them to my chest without realizing, and the soft wisps twirled along my fingers. The sword at my waist buzzed and shook inside its sheath. It responded to my panic as the memories arose and was trying its best to ease them.

"Thank you," I told it. The pain was deeper than a few strands of smoke could reach, but the distraction worked.

Erline was part of my past. I tried to avoid it; I killed the Providers as they came for me in Hallow's Promise, but I could never erase the years I spent at the king's right hand. I looked down at the dagger tattoo on my forearm for the first time in . . . a month. Since Valen had died and re-risen. The magic in the ink had faded once I'd used my powers again. As though the final connection had been waiting to be severed.

It was just a blade now. Not a chain.

A warm whisper rang in my ear.

"He's still looking for you, you know."

My spine straightened. I didn't turn, but I recognized Brynn's voice. She shifted, moving to my other side.

"His guards are swarming River's Edge. They interrogate all visitors who pass through the gates. Some of them never return." She stepped beside me, the bitter scent of burnt oil rolling from her cape. "It took me a long time to realize they were searching for anyone connected to . . . you. But then it was my turn."

Brynn moved to look at me. Her hood eclipsed half her face, bearing the other side to the light. Her eyes were red-rimmed, like she'd been crying. Her sweet, innocent face had thinned and turned harsh. I had missed those signs before, inside her shop. Had missed that look of fear buried deep.

"What did they do?" I asked. A vibration of anger settled low in my gut, and I forced it down. Whatever she said didn't excuse the choices she'd made—or the lives she'd taken.

"They questioned me for hours. They kept me in the dark and brought in people with powers more terrible than the next." Her gaze turned vacant. "My shop interested them. They knew you made potions and had to obtain supplies from somewhere. I admitted that you'd purchased from me before. I offered them anything if they'd let me go, let me live."

My throat bobbed. The king was more cunning than I gave him credit. He'd strangled the economy of Hallow's Promise and sat outside the walls while citizens searched elsewhere for a valuable coin. Then he exploited them in their weakness.

"I told them how to get through the walls. In return, they

let me go, with the vow to return the next week and the next, always demanding more from me."

"There was never a second store in River's Edge," I said softly.

"No. There were only pain and threats."

And there it was. Brynn had suffered because of me. The town was suffering because I had decided to hide here, and I decided to bring Valen back to life. Leof had tried to warn me. He knew the consequences would be sharp and severe.

I hadn't listened.

"I'm sorry," I whispered.

Brynn spun on me and grabbed my arm. I didn't move to stop her. My feet felt grounded in the soft dirt.

"You should be," she hissed. "I had *nothing*. No money, no inventory, no customers. Nothing except determination. I found a new market—one thirsty for anything I could provide."

"The animals."

"Exactly. Healing properties, magical powers, special abilities—any creature with a hint of magic gets the highest price on the black market. In the few short weeks I started collecting my inventory, my income soared. I had enough money to pay off the Providers in River's Edge to leave me alone. Once they had enough information and coins, they lost interest. By then, I'd gotten used to the wealth. I couldn't go back."

"Toren? Eleric? Did they get in your way?"

She laughed, a harsh, humorless sound. "Toren decided to grow a conscious. He couldn't sell the wyvern egg, even after all the trouble it was to kill the mother. He planned to raise it for his own. Can you imagine the questions he'd get if he started walking around with a baby wyvern? He'd spill my name as soon as the first constable questioned him."

"And once we suspected Eleric, he became a mess you needed to clean up."

"Exactly." Her eyes widened and danced in the light. Dy's voice groaned on and on. Valen was invisible in the crowd, which was what he had planned. I suddenly wished our plan was working a little less well now.

"Why did you come then? You must have known it was a trap."

"Of course I did. I planned to flee to Erline and never look back. I figured helping the Providers earned me enough clout to appeal to the king for aid."

I snorted. It probably earned her enough for a shallow grave—maybe.

She continued, "But when I heard about this auction, I realized there's another option. I have contacts here. The Siren's Sorrow is a goldmine of people looking to buy and trade any goods—alive or not. If I got rid of you, everything would go back to normal."

"You know that won't happen."

"Sure it will. The marshal has a suspect. He won't look at me, no matter how much your little friend insists. Who knows, maybe she'll have an accident, too. I have plenty of my sulfur mix left after Toren's . . . incident."

I clenched my hands into fists. The crowd roared as Dy's auction began to wind down. Someone was going to be very disappointed about the warplog they were certainly *not* taking home tonight.

Assuming we all survived.

"You won't leave here, Brynn."

"That's the thing, Rae. After we killed mama wyvern, I took its skin and painstakingly assembled every plucked scale into this." She pulled back her cloak, exposing a skin-tight ensemble that wrapped around her body. "Do you know what's special about wyverns?" She winked. "They're fireproof."

I screamed as Brynn threw something from her cloak pocket. My sword cleared the sheath, smoke already pouring from the blade, but Byrnn had backed away.

Moments later, a rim of fire sprouted around us, around all the auction attendees. Heat spread along my skin. The flames consumed the grass and leaves, unconcerned about the lingering cold or snow. They inched toward us, eager to burn.

And Brynn stood in the flames and laughed.

Chapter 24

"Sunshine." Valen grabbed my arm. "In case you haven't noticed, everything is on fire."

"Wow, no way. Thanks for telling me, I was planning to stand here and *die*."

He glanced down at me. Even in imminent death, a spark danced in his eyes. "That's certainly what it looks like."

I pulled my arm from his grasp. People around us screamed and ran, only to barge into the barrier of flames and repeat the process. Heat soaked into my clothes as the fire chipped away at the foliage beneath us. Their panic was contagious. My pulse thundered in my throat, and the hot air crawled into my lungs. It was so hot, too hot.

"We have to get to Bubbles," I said. "He doesn't like fire." Since we were almost burned alive inside Brew, Bubbles avoided getting too close to the popping embers of any fire. Sure, he didn't miss an opportunity for a cozy nap before the hearth, but he always eyed it wearily before settling down.

"Rae." My name on his lips sounded like a curse—or a plea. It sucked me out of the tunnel of panic and pushed me into the present. "I will get Bubbles, but you're our only hope for everyone to make it out of this alive."

I shook my head. Sweat pooled across my forehead. The surrounding smoke turned thicker, and not because of the swirls pouring from my sword.

None of my knowledge applied here. When the fire had threatened me and Bubbles last time, I had all my potion stocks available. I'd wielded a transformation spell and changed the flames into a monster that devoured the man who tried to kill us.

This time, I had nothing.

"I don't know what to do."

Valen cupped my face. His calmness spilled over into me. "You Captivated the House Spider. Now find something that can put out these flames."

And he was gone.

I sank to my knees. People screamed as the space shrank. Distantly, Brynn continued to laugh through the chaos. She could walk right out of the fire thanks to her wyvern armor, and decided to watch us all die instead.

The panic slowly ebbed, rage finding its place. I didn't want to Captivate anything, ever again. The spider had wanted to serve me—I became its joy. That feeling left a thick layer of grime inside my head.

But I also didn't want to cook to death.

I dug my fingers into the ground. The damp earth anchored me. I ducked my head and ignored the streaks of sweat as they spilled into my eyes. My magic, finally loosening like a muscle stretched after years of unuse, shaped into a spear and stabbed at the ground.

Beads of light spread. Each tiny flicker was a piece of life hunkered in the safety of The Void. I found one pulsing beat and focused on it. An image sharpened in my mind, a fragment of my imagination based on what the magic told me.

A turdle—basically a reptilian gopher, and not at all able to extinguish a fire.

The power eased from the turdle and searched again. More and more creatures appeared in the mental map, and I discarded them one after another.

Gods, the heat. I pulled my fingers from the dirt and fumbled with the button on my cloak. It fell from my shoulders, but there was no relief among the heated air. My shirt was soaked through with crusted sweat, and the sharp smoke had thickened as it burned more fuel. The others cried, huddling into each other, craving comfort while they died.

Died.

My power uncoiled as the first touch of death neared. Ah, it felt so sweet, the promises and potential of all this death.

I wanted to soak it in, to revel in its soft touches. If someone inside this hellish circle died, I could consume their deathly power. It would protect me from the flames. They could die, but I would live forever.

I deserved that.

My magic had only brought me pain and suffering. It was a target painted on my back the moment I had been born. My parents died because of it. My life was upheaved, and my childhood was painful. The least it could do was save my life—save me from the flames inching even closer.

Die, my magic whispered—to anyone. *Die, so I may live.*

A flash of movement parted the crowd. Across the pulse of people, Valen's face solidified through a small gap between bodies. A little—okay, not so little—green body cradled softly in his arms. My view of Bubbles was obstructed, but one tiny, dismayed croak echoed through the cracks of fire.

Oh no. No way my warplog was going to die tonight.

I yelled, letting the rage and frustration and fear seep into my voice. I forced all my unruly magic into a point and thrust it into the ground as I sank my hands into the dirt again. The magic didn't rebel—it couldn't. It was mine, damn it, and I was tired of its disobedience.

The lights of life illuminated again. I sought and discarded them one by one. The head drew closer. Someone collapsed, their pulse of life fading dangerously.

One bright flicker attracted my magic.

Yes, that was perfect.

The Void had given this creature power and sustained its wild magic with its own. I severed the strings. My magic bent to my will effortlessly. It felt natural—not as forced and heavy as trying to revive the dead bug days ago. No, it blended the fragmented ties of this creature into my power life force effortlessly.

And the being became mine.

Valen appeared. He shifted Bubbles into one hand and put the other on my shoulder. His knees shook. The flames would soon consume us all.

"Anytime, Sunshine," he said, but his words were whispers. Blisters danced along the back of the hand cradling the warplog. He'd touched the flames, probably trying to see if escape was possible.

"It's coming," I answered.

For what felt like hours, but must have been seconds, nothing happened. Valen's knees shook and he collapsed beside me. He pressed his sweaty forehead against mine. The touch of his power against my skin felt cool, but it was an illusion. No raw magic could defend a natural force like this.

"Sunshine," he said. His voice was weak.

"It's . . . coming," I gasped. The air was too hot. I was cooking from the inside out. People were fainting with the heat, the smoke inhalation, and over all of it, Brynn laughed.

The ground shook.

Valen lifted his head. His crystal eyes clarified as the earth rattled with each step my creature took.

"You didn't."

A terrible roar cut across the tops of the trees. It burrowed into my ears, and if I had the strength to cover them, I would have. Nobody screamed or yelled—we were too defeated by the heat about to claim our lives.

The monster burst through the trees. A horrible being, its back brushed against the top of the tallest trees. Thick, blue scales wrapped its body, and the smell of bog followed in its wake. Four round feet pummeled the earth as each step forced it to succumb to the monster's will.

A swamp dragon.

It wasn't really a dragon, not in the official sense. Its true name was Large Draxton Salamander, but everyone called them swamp dragons. They preferred to rest in the depths of still lakes—the colder the better—and only emerged once every century for eating and breeding. The Creature Husbandry and Welfare unit, directed by Erline, carefully monitored most of the swamp dragon lakes. They liked to warn locals when the beast would emerge to minimize human casualties.

But the CHW had missed this one.

It roared again, then turned its massive head to study the ring of fire. I felt the unhappiness that its new life source—me—was about to be killed. It wanted to protect me, both because of the sudden bond between us and because it wanted to live. Some instinctual part of the monster recognized my demise equaled its own.

A low gurgle built at the base of the creature's throat. Its body quivered and shook, and the noise grew. I preferred the deafening roar, to be honest, over the pulsing sloshing sounds.

"Is it going to—"

Valen didn't finish his sentence.

The swamp dragon burped and expelled the largest chunk of slime out of its mossy mouth. The thick wad sailed toward us in a beautiful, rainbow arch of bubble and spit trails. I spotted the distinct outline of a fish before that wonderful, disgusting fluid splashed onto us.

It was thick, and it smelled terrible. Definitely sharp and vile, like vomit, but also cool and refreshing as the flames smothered almost immediately. It coated my skin with slime. I savored the feeling. Anything was better than that suffocating heat.

Valen wiped his eyes and flicked a thick glob onto the ground. He sent me a glare.

"Of all the choices, you pick the swamp dragon?"

I shrugged. "That's a weird way to thank me for saving your life."

"Please." He staggered to his knees. Some of the color returned to his face, giving him a softer, calmer glow. "We both know you were saving *his* life." He thrust Bubbles toward me, and I scooped the warplog into my arms. He studied me and licked one eyeball.

People groaned. The swamp monster's slime cooled quicker than water alone. Some helped others to their feet, but more simply disappeared into the dark. Those betting on an animal at an illegal midnight auction weren't usually the heroic type.

Speaking of which . . .

Brynn stared at the scene. The carefully orchestrated mess she'd designed had swiftly fallen apart. Her eyes widened and her mouth opened and closed. She finally saw me and our gazes locked.

"Don't!" I yelled.

Too late.

Brynn turned and ran.

Chapter 25

Valen and I watched her figure fade into the darkness.

"Aren't you going to go after her?" Valen asked.

I glanced around and pointed a finger at myself. "Me? You know I don't run."

That earned me a snort. "I can't run right now, either. I'm fairly certain there are blisters on my feet."

"Don't worry. I know someone who can."

I mentally tugged on the magic connecting me and the swamp dragon. The earth pulsed again as it swung its giant head toward the direction Brynn had run. Its steps echoed through the darkness. A moment later, a woman screamed.

"Is it eating her?"

I sighed. "Unfortunately, it's just incapacitating her until we can get over there."

"Decapitation is an effective form of incapacitation."

"And I'm sure you know that from experience, but I need Brynn alive. Her story will set Celeste free and show Castor the error of his ways."

Valen wrapped an arm around my waist and drew me closer. He pressed a kiss to the top of my head, which sent streaks of warmth—good warmth, not the kind that wanted to cook me—all the way to the bottom of my toes.

"I love you," he breathed.

I looked up at him and studied the blue deposits in his eyes, how they shifted from darker to lighter and flickered when he looked at me.

"I love you, too."

* * *

The next morning, I set the swamp monster free. Valen and I stood near the lake in the center of The Void while the being sank into the murky depths. My magic rebuilt the connections with the forest, and a peace fell over the place when the creature returned to its slumber.

A part of it still echoed in my mind. It was content to be back in its home.

And I felt terrible for taking it away in the first place.

"Am I . . . bad?" I asked.

Valen tensed. His arm around me turned unnaturally still.

"Why would you ask that?"

I shrugged. "This is the second creature I've forced to do my will. My presence has caused Hallow's Promise to turn against Erline and lose all economic support. If they questioned Brynn while she was outside the walls, that means others are being questioned, too. How many need to be interrogated because of me before it's my fault?" There was more—that Providers entered the city and threatened those I loved. That Leof was basically in charge of an entire rebel faction. That Brynn may never have turned to committing crimes if her business hadn't collapsed.

But my throat closed, and my tongue stuck. Tears pooled in my eyes.

"I can't keep everyone safe," I said. "They might be better if I . . . just gave up."

Valen pulled me close. "Rae, nobody is safe. The concept is an illusion. The truth is, bad things happen in this world. All you can do is be with the people you love and cherish the moments you have. And I do."

"You do what?" I wiped my eyes.

"I cherish every moment I have with you."

I let his strong arms pull me close. He still smelled like slime and swamp, but also of life. His heart beat in my ear. I'd once lived without hearing that sound—and I'd never let that happen again.

So, we held each other. Two broken people caught in a broken war, with only love and stubbornness to see us through.

* * *

"I appreciate everything you did, Rae. I'm not expecting anything more." Celeste's voice was clear and confident as we walked down Main Street side by side.

The look on Castor's face when Brynn told him everything had been worth almost cooking to death. His cheeks had bulged out, and his eyes got impossibly wide. It had taken everything in me not to laugh in his face. Hopefully, he learned a valuable lesson—that he was wrong, and I was always right.

"Just hear me out first, then you can decide your next step. I want you to know all your options."

She rubbed her hands. "I've been away too long already. My father is very frail—he can't take care of himself."

"Who are you calling frail?" Mr. Haverhill's hands shook as he gripped a wooden cane tightly in one hand. I eyed the stick suspiciously. I was pretty sure he carried it as a weapon rather than a walking aid.

Celeste froze. "Dad?"

He huffed, but an edge of silver lined his eyes. Celeste ran into his arms, and he hugged her back so tightly that it confirmed my suspicions about the cane.

"I'm glad everything got cleared up." His voice was rough, as though unused to speaking, but the truth was genuine. "I don't know what I would have done without you, Celeste."

"Oh, hush dad." She wiped away her own tears. "You would have been fine." She turned over her shoulder and looked at me. "Why is my father here?"

"Typical," he gruffed. "Never 'thank the gods my father is here.'"

They laughed and I chuckled.

"Your father and I talked while the final paperwork for your release was prepared. We have an offer that you may be interested in."

Her expression froze and shifted, turning suspicious. "What kind of offer?" Caution lined her voice.

I stepped around the pair, beneath the overhang of the door in front of us. It had been repainted in the hours since I'd released the swamp monster—turquoise blue to represent the creature that freed us all.

And the name had been repainted. The silver letters of Dollups and Dashes had been permanently erased, changed into—

"Celeste's Serendipity?" She eyed the sign I'd hastily made. "What does that mean?"

Mr. Haverhill nudged her with the end of his stick. "It means, girl, that you can finally get out of the butcher business."

"There's been a sudden vacancy in this store and with the economic climate, the town can't afford to keep a high-profile location empty. We still need access to all these supplies and with your contacts outside the walls, you'd be able to keep inventory on the shelves." I fixed the sign, which had sagged on one end. "A real war is approaching. It will take everything we have to keep Hallow's Promise alive. Having a flow of supplies available will aid in those efforts. But only if you want to."

She eyed the shop. Every emotion played across her face, but the final look was uneasy longing.

"I don't know," she said. "My dad worked so hard on his shop. I . . . I need to support him."

He whacked her with the cane.

"Ouch!" Celeste rubbed her head. "Dad!"

"You gave up everything when we lost your mother." There wasn't sympathy in his tone, no, only strength. "I'm retired and damn well don't want to move in my old age. You taking this shop and supplying this city makes sure I die exactly where I want to—in my own damn bed."

Celeste rolled her eyes. "Thanks for the motivational speech, Dad, they're always the best." She bit her lip. "But if you're sure . . . Then, yes, I'd love to accept this shop. I-I really don't know how to repay you."

I squeezed her arm and handed over the keys. "Chuck the sulfur. I never want to see any of that stuff ever again."

We laughed and talked for a few more minutes, then I left

Celeste and her father and ventured back home.

Chapter 26

We gathered around my little kitchen counter. Valen, Krissa, Ilene, Bubbles, me, and Whiskers. The tension had eased. We'd survived the fire and had cleared Celeste's name. I finished filtering out the chunky parts of my homemade mead and dividing the batch between mugs for everyone to enjoy.

A whine emitted from the other side of the house. Ilene jerked straight.

"The chalice," she said and launched from the group to attend to the cup where someone was attempting to scry her from the war effort. Valen swiped her mug as she disappeared and dumped the contents into his own glass with a wink.

"You did it," he said.

"Of course she did it." Krissa rolled her eyes so hard, I thought they might stick that way. "She's the best. In fact, you probably slowed her down. I bet she could have done it all faster if you'd stayed away."

Valen winked again. "I have to agree with that."

"Yes, really, because she wouldn't have to pull—" Krissa trailed off and squinted at Valen. The mercenary raised his glass in a silent salute. "I didn't think you'd agree with me. But good. Because I'm right."

I smiled as I sipped. The mead was sweet and cool. I wasn't ready for anything hot yet, not while the memories of my skin burning were so recent. Soon, I'd take Brew, and we'd go sell some delicious hot teas to the people of Hallow's Promise.

But not tonight.

A few concerning noises rose above our quiet conversation. Ilene's people often called in the thick of a battle for advice or strategies. The clang of sword fighting and screams were a normal part of her calls.

A sharp cracking sound followed. I flinched.

"What did Castor say when you brought Brynn in?" Krissa's shoulders sagged while she worked on the mead. The tension had been impacting everyone. We needed this time together to unwind.

"After a few select curses, he finally said, 'Not bad, witch.'" And I think that was the best compliment Castor would ever give me. "He seemed more impressed by the swamp dragon outside the station and that I threatened that he'd get eaten if he didn't listen to me."

Krissa laughed. The sound was pure, unfiltered.

My heart swelled. I loved everyone here so much. We'd seen the worst in the world and repeatedly decided to stand up again—for ourselves and each other.

The cracking sound came again. A few moments later, Ilene rejoined the circle.

Her face was white.

"I have news from the front lines," she said. "The king is pulling all his soldiers from the northern battle. Every Erline sworn sword is retreating."

"That's good, right?" Krissa's voice held a brittle hope, like she already knew the answer.

Ilene and Valen shared a glance.

"It is not good," the Scourge of Erline said. "There are very few reasons the king would abandon this front."

"He plans to create a new one," Valen chimed in.

"Here," I said. It was my voice, but I didn't hear the words. My heart stopped. "The king is bringing the war to Hallow's Promise."

Ilene studied me with a gaze strikingly similar to Valen's. "I am afraid so. I'd hoped you would have more time to prepare before this happened, but our timelines will have to shift. We need your magic. It will be the only way to win, to survive."

My throat closed. Krissa grabbed my hand, and I squeezed her fingers. "I will do everything I can." My magic twisted, slightly looser, a bit more responsive than before. That would be enough—it had to be.

She turned to her brother. Gone was the loving sister, replaced by the general that life had forced Ilene to become.

"We need the stone, Nightwrath."

And just like that, Valen was gone, too. A cold, battle-hardened warrior stood in his place.

And I loved him, too.

"I will find it."

"Good. If the Oracle does not provide insight into the king's strategies, then this will be lost very quickly. Prepare your supplies and spread the word—war is approaching." Ilene blinked a few times, as though coming out of a trance. She turned a bit, revealing something small and soft nestled in the crook of her armored arm. "Also, this emerged from the fireplace. I believe it hatched from the egg Rae was cooking."

I blinked, too. Our jaws dropped as the tiny being wrapped two oversized wings around its body and nestled its little head deeper into Ilene's arm. The metal plates and bloody spots didn't seem to deter the baby from its slumber.

The cracking sounds . . . hadn't been from the front lines.

It had been the baby wyvern hatching.

The silence lasted for another second, then Krissa broke it. Despite the war at our heels and how our lives had irreparably changed in a matter of seconds, she spoke what we were all thinking at that moment.

"Awwwwww."

❋ ❋ ❋

FREE BONUS CHAPTER Sneak Peak

The golden throne pushed against the king's tender muscles. His silken robes, spun with strands of material to match the color of his throne, did little to soften the hard seat. Even the crown atop his head weighed down his neck, and he strained to keep his spine straight.

The damn disease. Every day it sank deeper through his body. He'd gone through two more necromancers since discovering Drayven's location in that cursed village. They all cried and begged for mercy, but when given the option between killing another or losing their own lives, they always chose to save themselves. Their powers, however, didn't come close to Drayven's, leaving the king weaker by the day.

He needed her. There were no other options....

WANT MORE?

Free BONUS chapter for newsletter subscribers only!
Click the link, visit my website (anpayton.com), or scan the
QR code below:

Want to Support the Author?

The easiest way is to leave a review on your favorite reading platform. Reviews help us get visibility in the community, and spread our books to a wider audience.

Whether or not you choose to leave a review, THANK YOU for being here and reading our books.

Acknowledgments

A huge thank you to all the usuals:

- Nicole at The Assist, LLC - thank you for always encouraging my characters, even if they're a little crazy
- GetCovers for another collaborative cover creation center
- My husband and kids for literally everything - you are my biggest supporters!

Most of all, thank you to all the readers out there waiting for the next book, and the next. Rae's adventure has meant so much to me, personally, and I'm amazed that so many others are following her journey. THANK YOU!!

About the Author

A.N. Payton is a fantasy romance author, true-crime obsessee, and a very low-skilled seamstress. She writes at the intersection of fantasy and science, with a dash (or overflowing scoop) of romance. Her books are concocted with the perfect proportions of strong female characters, sexy men who may or may not end up shirtless, and plenty of sarcastic banter.

A.N. Payton spends her days at a top-secret job (if she told you, she'd have to kill you), which proves real life is more wild than fiction. At night she escapes by writing new worlds and problems for someone else to solve - probably with a sword.

She lives in the pacific northwest with a husband she loves (depending on the day), two kids she loves (most of the time), and a dog she loves (all the time).

Other Works by A.N. Payton

Princess Sal's magic bought her people peace and security, but she'll never be safe with the vampire king in her castle.

Centuries of war come to a bitter end when Princess Sal's parents steal half the witch army and disappear. Sal is forced to surrender to the vampire king, Kadence, and bind her magic as part of their agreement. She will give anything to protect her people – anything except her heart.

When Kadence conquers the witch kingdom, he doesn't expect their princess to be as delicious as wild honey. He can't decide if he'd rather kiss or kill Sal, and his desire for her battles against his hatred of witches. Despite their attraction, Kadence can't forget their war-torn history. He must decide if he can overcome his past to make way for a new future – one that might include Sal.

But when scouts locate Sal's parents and discover they're marching a demon army toward the kingdom, Sal and Kadence must unite their people for a final battle. If they don't, bloodthirsty demons will consume everyone they vowed to protect. Can they work together to save their people, or will hellfire destroy them all?